DELUSION
THE LOVE OF MY LIFE

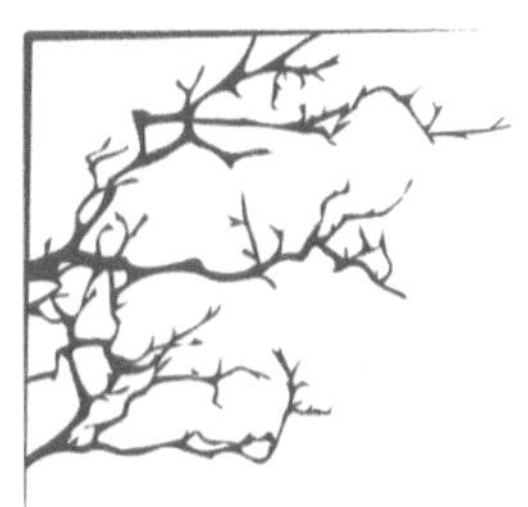

By
Wayne Clark

Cover designed by Wayne Clark

I wrote this book because I wanted to follow my dreams even though I suffer from dyslexia. It has been tough to write this, but I finally achieved what I wanted to do with great support. I have done so many things, but this is the best I have ever done in my life. I want to say a big thank you to Nicole Glozier, my wife to be for her encouragement.

DELUSION
THE LOVE OF MY
LIFE

CHAPTER ONE

You must know, all I wanted from the very beginning was for her to be happy. In my mind, it seemed too simple - but then again, things are rarely as simple as they seem. I wanted her to smile when she saw me, I wanted her to laugh at my bad jokes, and I wanted her to be happy when she was around me. I wanted her to be mine. Again, things are rarely as simple as you'd think they'd be. The first time I saw her, I knew instantly that she was meant for me. I'd never felt anything like what I experienced as I watched her jogging down the sidewalk that day. She was brighter than the sun and as striking as a lightning bolt. Her long, straight, dark-blonde hair blew in the breeze, and it was almost as if I could feel its tendrils snaring me in their trap. She only wore a yellow sports bra and yoga pants. Her flawless tan skin begged me to touch it. I knew that this is what people called love at first sight. It was more substantial than anything I had felt before. The need to talk to her and be next to her was almost all-consuming.

Yet, I couldn't make my legs move. I was glued to the spot, there in the parking lot with full grocery bags dangling from my hands. She kept jogging, and my eyes followed her every move. She was graceful, even out of breath, with sweat dripping from her brow. And then she was gone, out of sight. I knew I had a goofy smile on my face as I carried my groceries into my apartment. I felt butterflies in my stomach, but my heart was aching. I wondered if I'd ever get the chance to see her again. Had I let her walk out of my life just as fast as she had walked into it? Had I missed my opportunity? I made a split decision, grabbing my keys from where I had just put them down and got back into my car. It had only been a few minutes; indeed, I could catch up with her. I drove around the apartment complex's parking lot, hoping and praying that I could find her before she went inside, and I lost her. My prayers were mercifully answered as I caught sight of her unlocking a door to an apartment. My heart pounded like a drum. I pulled into a parking space a few cars down from where she stood and then got out. Her door closed behind her, and suddenly, I was so nervous I felt like I was going to puke. My palms were clammy, and my fingers shook.

I slowly made my way up to her door, and then I stood there, wondering what I would say to her. That's when I heard the chorus of a popular indie rock song, I listened to it a few times on the radio, and then I could hear her sweet voice as she answered the phone. My heart may have skipped a beat.

"Hey, sorry I didn't answer the first time; I was on my run."

The muffled voice from the inside took my breath away. She was so beyond perfect. She could have been an angel on earth.

"Yeah, I know what you mean," she continued and then giggled. The sound of her laugh was like a bell.

"Tonight?" a note to surprise in her voice.

"That's kind of short notice, Kate."

I listened intently, not wanting to miss a single word.

"I mean, when have I ever turned down one of her crazy parties? Of course, I'm going!"

I felt a little shock in my veins. Was she going to a party tonight? That would be the perfect time to introduce myself. Admittedly, it seemed a little weird to meet her right now, just as a stranger randomly knocking at her door, and I knew what I was doing was wrong, but I couldn't help myself. I felt like a creep.

"Okay, I'll be there around eight. Okay. Love you too, Kate."

She giggled, and then she was off the phone.

I hurried back to my car, not wanting to be seen quite yet. I debated whether I should go home and get ready and then come back or if I should wait here in the parking lot until she left. I didn't want to miss her leaving because otherwise, I wouldn't know where to go. After a few minutes, I returned to my apartment to get ready. I was sweaty, wearing a faded tee shirt and dirty jeans. I had to make a good impression for meeting the possible love of my life.

Wait... did I say that? I guess this may well be the love of my life. I got ready and was back parked in front of her apartment within an hour, and from there, it was only about a thirty-minute wait until she walked out of her apartment dressed in a short gold dress and high heels, holding a clutch purse in her hand. My mouth dropped open seeing her in that outfit. Her hair was curled now, and her makeup was beautiful.

She looked like a goddess. I watched her get into a small newer model silver car and start it up.

I waited for her to get farther down the road before I followed. I didn't want to be seen quite yet. I followed at a safe distance to the outskirts of town, where we arrived at a massive house with thumping music blaring from every window. There were people everywhere. It was hard to find a parking spot on the congested street, so I had to park in this small field off-road.

I investigated the rear-view mirror to make sure no one had spotted me where I parked, and it seemed I was safe.

Yet, I still sat in my car, nervous about what I might say to her. I kept checking my appearance in the rear-view mirror while practicing my speech for when I finally approached her. My heart was sure pounding at the thought of talking to her for what would be the first time. I took a deep breath before getting out of my car. I opened the car door and placed one leg out, but as I did, a man slammed his hand on top of my car roof and shouted,

"YOU CAN'T PARK HERE, PRICK."

He was slurring his words mouthing off like some drunk teenager.

"Okay... I'll move my car then. I don't want any trouble."

I couldn't get a clear look at him because he was wearing a grey hooded jacket and his hood was up. He was too drunk, and I doubt he owns this field for a minute. They weren't anywhere I could park, so I pulled out my wallet and took out ten bucks, hoping he would take it and leave me alone.

"Ah... you can park here... I tell you what... if you throw me another ten, I could look after your car?" he asks, slurring his words.

I couldn't blame him for making a little cash out of me. Nonetheless, I took out another ten and said,

"Just take this and clear off."

He took the cash and walked off with no bother at all. Yet, I stood there checking my appearance in my side mirror for the last time. I suppose this will have to do. I turned around facing the house when I saw a group of people in the front yard dancing, shouting, and getting into all kinds of bother.

I casually strolled across the street towards the house while carefully watching my surroundings. But as I walked closer to the house, I saw the love of my life walking out the front door, yapping on her cell phone. I walked over while playing it cool, mixing in with others until she finished her phone call, but I stood eavesdropping on her conversation. I listened to her every word.

"Where the hell are you, Kate? But you said you would be here before me. Fine. Don't be too long, okay?"

I was a few feet away from her. I could smell her to the point I needed to get close to her. I was tempted to walk up close so I could smell her. That's when I slowly coated towards her where she stood.

I was about to speak to her, but some big shot decided to beat me to it. I couldn't bear it. The thought of them both together.

I felt gutted, hurt, and betrayed because that was to be the love of my life. I watched as they both chatted away with each other. She gave him a look that should have been mine and not for him. She gently took his hand and pulled him into the house. At that point, I had to remain calm.

"Come with me," she says while holding that same look.

I followed them both into the house when I saw them walking up the stairs giggling. The house was like a drug den. That's when I could see a couple on the bottom of the stairs making out. I'm not sure if this was a house party or a swinger's club?

My heartbeat was twice the average rate it should have because I knew what was about to happen. I waited until they were both out of sight so I could follow them. I need to get drunk to calm my nerves. That's when a guy walks in the house holding an entire bottle of whisky. I took it right from his hands.

"I'll have that."

I gulp it back in one.

"HEY, THAT'S MINE."

I burp like a pig.

"Piss off before I do something I won't regret."

After that, I slowly made my way up the stairs when I heard moaning and groaning. I craned my head to pinpoint precisely where they were. I followed the sound to the bathroom door. I leaned down and began peeking through the keyhole to witness my love leaning over the bathtub with her skirt pulled up to her waistline and her knickers down to her ankles, reviling him inside of her. I felt angry but turned on by the thought of it being me in his shoes. But the realization of it was terrifying as it wasn't me.

"I want to feel you deep inside me," she begs.

I couldn't bear it any longer. I needed to end this as soon as possible, but how? I stood up, pacing up and down outside the bathroom door. Yet, I could still hear them fucking. It was driving me **CRAZY!** Even the sound of the music from downstairs couldn't block out the groaning sounds coming from her. I took one last look to see him thrusting her deeper. Truth was... I was powerless to stop them. I decided to head back downstairs and wait for them to finish.

I sat on the couch talking with a random middle-aged guy with dark, short ratty hair. He was wearing biker leathers. He spoke of how easy most women were here, but I wasn't interested. The only woman I wanted was upstairs fucking some guy. I couldn't care what this guy was chatting about as long as he continued to pass the drinks, then I would continue to listen... almost, listening.

Time passed thirty minutes exactly. The love of my life came staggering through the living room. She was clearly off her face. I hoped she wasn't planning on driving home in her state. The guy who just fucked her came into the living room, quickly picked up his jacket, and left in a hurry. Maybe I should go over and speak with her? My heart said yes, but my mind said no. I sat there in silence as she danced away to the sound of the music. I watched her every move. I even imagined her looking at me while she dances. She moved so sexily. Her eyes were closed as she moved to every single beat of that song. I knew I could not intrude right now.

Yet, I felt stupid. I didn't catch her name, but I would love to know her name. I could sit here all night and watch her dance. My eyes gaze across the room. I could see her purse and cell phone on the side just by the door as you walk in... stupid to leave your personal belongings just lying around for some random person to pick up. I stood from sitting on the couch and casually walked over to her personal belongings. I picked up her cell phone and purse and walked over to her, and said,

"Hi."

She slowly opened her eyes and made eye contact. The most beautiful look I was waiting for... but she suddenly looked at her belongings that were resting in the palm of my hands and said,

"WHY ARE YOU TOUCHING MY STUFF?" she asks. She raised her right eyebrow. I didn't know what to say. I paused momentarily, thinking of what to say, but I was lost for words, and every voice in the room hovered over me like a dozen drones. The only thing I did say was,

"I..." I was tripping over words again; she had gotten to me, and she could tell.

She snatched her purse and cell phone from my hands and said,

"Don't even think of arguing back," she firmly went on.

I stood almost paralyzed at the brutal hostility coming from her.

"Okay... I was simply bringing your belongings to you before someone steals them,"

"You need a mental health day, a long weekend."

I played it cool, took it in my stride, apologized to her, gave her a polite nod, and briefly smiled. Yet, she walked off, and I stood there in the middle of the living room floor as I watched her walk out of my life again. Nonetheless, she left, so I followed her but headed back to my car to follow her home, ensuring she got home safely. I couldn't bear the thought of anything happening to her, especially while she was drunk. I wouldn't forgive myself if anything did happen to the love of my life.

CHAPTER TWO

I hadn't slept most of the night; I pulled into the same parking space across the street from where she lives. I stayed there all night, but I knew I couldn't keep doing that. I need a way I can keep my eye on her... I couldn't knock on her door, especially after what she said to me... maybe she needs more time? I sat there with a few scenarios in my head and came up with one idea... A few cameras around her home. It made perfect sense to me. I would never miss her leaving the house, and I could understand her more. I need to study her. As they say... it's always best to work a woman out before approaching them, and this just seemed like the best possible way. My head told me this was all wrong, but my heart was saying differently, and she is the love of my life. She needs to embrace that. I switched on the engine and drove back to my apartment. I pulled up outside my apartment, went back inside, and went through my old computer stuff still packed up inside a box.

I never really had the time to use it, so I kept it packed away. So, there I was, searching through the box. They were a keyboard, monitor, and almost everything, including a few wireless cameras, which I could use with my cell phone instead of a computer. I wasn't sure of their range, but I was going to find out. I took the wireless cameras, picked up my car keys where I left them last, and walked straight out the door. I walked over to my car, got inside, and drove back to her place. I waited and waited for her to leave her apartment to sneak inside and plant the cameras somewhere, but it seemed like I was waiting forever!

Yet, as time passed, it was ten o'clock at night. She still hadn't left her apartment, but every light in her apartment was off.

I decided to look at her apartment complex to see if they were any way I could get inside and quickly plant the cameras and leave.

After looking around, I saw an open window to her apartment. It was a hot night, so that was the perfect opportunity to get inside. I climbed through the small open window to her bathroom while carefully watching my surroundings. It was quiet and not a sound in the air. I was sneaking around to see where she was. I wanted to see her again. I needed to see her. I was sneaking around her apartment when I saw her lying asleep on her bed wearing nothing but a pair of black silk knickers. My heart pounded at the thought of me lying next to her while she slept. Her breasts were amazingly smooth-looking C-cup. She looked so peaceful too.

Yet, I gazed around her room and saw a chair in the corner just by her wardrobe. I walked over to the chair and picked it up, placing it at the side of her bed. I took a seat and watched her as she peacefully slept.

I watched her for almost an hour. I was sitting there thinking about my life with her, thinking about what could be or what will be. Nonetheless, after watching her, I decided to look around her room to see where I could place at least one camera... in between two books? No... that's too obvious. But my eyes rested the longest on the top of her wardrobe. I could easily place it there, pointing down. The bags on top would give it an incredible hide, and I knew she wouldn't go up there because the amount of dust shows she hardly cleans there.

After placing the camera on top of the wardrobe, I walked back to her, watching her sleep. I was tempted to touch her. I wanted to feel her. I guess temptation got the better of me. I stood over her and ran my fingertips gently between her breasts and then slowly down to her bikini line.

She was silky smooth as she looked. She is everything I ever dreamed of. Yet, after admiring her body, I went back to my car and sat on the driver's side. I took out my cell phone to set the camera's resolution. Perfect. I switched camera feeds to make sure they worked correctly, and they did.

The following day I had woken to the sound of a knock at my door. I leapt out of bed and answered the door in just my robe. A delivery guy stood before me and held out a parcel and said,

"Anthony?"

"That's me," I replied.

I took the parcel, signed for it, and shut the door in his face. I hate being woken by the sound of my door being knocked, so I'm not a nice guy when such a nasty thud wakes me. Nonetheless, it wasn't anything special but a light bulb for my fridge that I ordered a month ago. Why I ordered from China, I don't know. Every few weeks, the bulb blows out, so I usually order a batch each time. Thinking about that now, I could have just saved up for a new fridge.

Yet, I walked to the kitchen and checked the clock, and it was 9:15, and today, I had to go to work. It's not a great job being bossed around. I had to deal with stupid idiots every day, but it's a job, and it's only a few blocks away from where I live, and the money isn't bad either. I placed the parcel on the kitchen side, picked up my cell phone, and switched on the camera application, and there she was, sitting in her living room eating a bowl of cereal. She eats amazingly too.

I kissed my phone because that was the only way I could feel close to her, for now. Nonetheless, I took a quick shower, got in my work clothes, and went straight out the front door, locking it behind me. I gazed around as I heard a couple arguing in the street. I laughed as I watched them quietly argue over her husband or boyfriend, looking at another woman.

"If you liked her that much, why didn't you just get her number?"

"Honey, you got it wrong. Please just calm down!"

I laughed more challengingly as I walked over to my car. I opened my car door and sat in the driver's seat. That's when I switched on the camera application again. I overheard the love of my life on the phone; she says,

"You didn't show up at the party, Kate. I did get with someone, though. He was amazing. He called my name while fucking me over the bathtub; he goes. Oh, Laura, you're so good. ***Kate was in a rush***. Okay. Speak soon."

I felt hurt when I heard her talking with her friend, Kate. Kate may be a problem too. I did get her name, though... Laura. Yet, I sat there thinking about Laura and Kate. Maybe Kate is the one that encouraged her to sleep with this guy? I felt so angry that I punched the steering wheel about five times. I thought I was going crazy. I wanted Laura on her own, and I didn't want anyone in our way. I needed some kind of plan to kill Kate.

After thinking about how Kate should die, I wanted it to be up close and personal. Yet, I thought about strangling her, but even that was too quick. I looked at my cell phone for the last time before driving to work. The love of my life walks out of her apartment. I couldn't use my cell phone at that point.

That's when I switched on the engine and drove around the block to see if I could find her. I realized at this point I had lost her sight. I stopped my car just outside her apartment as I needed to search her apartment for clues. I needed Kate's address. I got out of my car and walked back to the same window as before. It was still wide open, luckily. I climbed inside and began my search, starting with her bedroom. I searched her bedside table, dresser, under the bed, and wardrobe, but nothing showed results. I went into the living room and walked over to her couch. Next to her couch was a small table. Her address book could be seen resting on it, just waiting for me to pick it up.

I picked it up and began to scan through it. After looking through the first three pages, I found it. *Gotcha*. I had Kate's name, address, and phone number. I even had her work address too. ***Result***. I tore out just that page and went back to my car and back to my apartment. I needed to think of my next move.

Later that day, around 9 pm, I was in my apartment going through scenarios. I was ready to end Kate's life. I picked up my car keys where I left them last, went back to my car, and drove to the outskirts of town to Kate's address. I took a steady left into St David's Road and slowly moved up the road to find Kate's house. Laura, at this point, was nowhere to be seen, so it gave me time to get rid of Kate once and for all. I can feel Laura, and we will be as one very soon. With Kate out of the picture, it shouldn't be a problem. Yet, after driving around, I saw a lady outside a house, alone, smoking a cigarette. ***Could this be Kate?***

I pulled up just across the street and switched off my engine. I hadn't a clue what Kate looked like. I waited until she went back inside. I needed to snoop around to see if anyone else was inside the house. Yet, I waited only ten minutes before she returned to the house. I reached for the glove box and took out a bottle of the nerve agent, enough to make her pass out. Never ask a killer where he gets his equipment.

I got out of my car and ran across the road before being seen. I walked through the front gate and down the short pathway. I then looked through the front window. I couldn't see anyone in the living room. That's when I walked around the back of her house and looked through the small square window to the kitchen. From what I could see, no one else was in that house apart from her. But how can I be so sure that this person was Kate? I quietly walked over to the back door and tried turning the door knob. It was unlocked. I sneaked into the kitchen and found a hiding place as now wouldn't be a good time to kill her. I needed to wait it out a little longer. I was hiding in the kitchen closet while sweating out all the same. Not the best place to hide.

Hours later, the sound of the house was as quiet as a graveyard. It was twelve-thirty in the morning, and at this point, I was desperate for a piss. I stepped out of the closet and began sneaking quietly around the house. First, I checked her mail on the kitchen side. It was the Kate I was looking for. I walked upstairs to find Kate fast asleep in bed. I placed a little nerve agent on a cloth and slowly walked up to her side of the bed. I stared hard, scared. My body felt numb and cold. I just thought of Laura and me being together. I slowly got on top of her, but she suddenly opened her eyes wide. She was about to scream. I quickly placed the cloth over her face while pinning her down, ensuring she couldn't get away or kick out. **I could not stop now.** Yet, I was feeling pleasure from this. She struggled a little and tried to kick out, but she slowly stopped kicking her legs and began to calm down after a while. She then passed out. I rolled off her and ran to the bathroom and threw up. After throwing up, I went to the sink to wash my hands and face. I looked in the mirror but hated the reflection staring back at me. Yet, guilt hit me like an uncontrollable raging storm. I'm not sure if it was too much adrenaline or the thought of what I had to do next.

CHAPTER THREE

That same night I was driving around with Kate in the boot of my car. I took her back to my cabin up in the mountains, just a few miles east of here. The house was in the middle of nowhere. It was dry and cold, like old raspy lungs, and I didn't need to worry about anyone driving or walking up that way unless they were planning to pay me a very unlikely visit, but if whoever did, it would be very thoughtful. I'm not a… make a friend type.

My father was my only friend before he passed away five years ago from a stroke. I will always miss him to this day. He would have been so proud. I drove up to the driveway and pulled up in front of the cabin. I stepped out of my car and walked around to the boot. But I heard branches cracking in the woods.

"Hello?" I call.

I had to be sure no one was around. Probably a stupid deer again. Nonetheless, I opened the boot and carefully dragged Kate out of the boot and into the cabin and down into the basement. I didn't know what I was going to do with her yet.

Hours later, I looked down at Kate, who was unconscious. I ran a gloved hand down her side with a smirk on my face.

"This is going to be fun."

Kate slowly blinked her eyes awake, at first not remembering where she was at or what happened. Then it all flooded back, and she gasped, looking around at her surroundings. She was strapped down with leather straps. She didn't know what was about to happen, and she didn't want to find out. She struggled a bit, but to no avail. She almost screamed after sighting all the different, huge torture devices around the room and mass amounts of old blood that could be seen on the walls, but it wasn't human blood. I used to hunt in the summer with my father and kill whatever moved in the woods for food. It was fun, I tell ya. She almost passed out upon seeing the old blood.

"Oh look, Kate is awake!"

I watched her as she began to shake. I lightly touched her chin, a grin spreading across my face. I wanted to make sure that this was Kate, so I asked,

"What's your name?"

Her voice trembled as she spoke.

"K-Kate. M-My N-name is Kate. Who, who a-are y-you?"

I chuckled darkly,

"You're not allowed to ask the questions around here. I do. But I'll let this one go. I am the one that will be a husband to your best friend." I grinned more at the thought of that. Kate gasped, then began struggling against the lather bonds keeping her down, but it was getting tighter no matter how hard she pulled and wriggled. I smirked and said,

"Ah, no escape for you. Don't make this worse for yourself."

A few tears came to Kate's eyes, and I laughed.

"Save your tears, princess. They don't bother me, whatsoever."

A small choke came from the back of Kate's throat.

"P-Please, don't d-do this. I-I'll give you anything..." her voice went into a tiny squeak,

"Please don't k-kill me."

I slowly grinned wide, then began to laugh lightly, and then my laugh became louder, making Kate cower.

"Don't kill you? Don't kill you? HA! As if!"

Kate was silent, except for the slight choking sounds coming from the back of her throat. She couldn't speak. Not a word. I laughed harder.

"You might want to save your breath; you're going to need it, I tell ya!"

I went over to the table, picked up a scalpel, and walked back to Kate.

"Don't worry. This will only hurt... a lot." I laughed; then went to examine Kate's body,

"Oh, wait, this is in the way."

I ripped off her shirt, making her whimper in response.

"Oh, don't worry about that old thing. You won't be needing it where you're going."

I put the scalpel to Kate's chest.

"Sweet, bloody, nightmares!" I cut deep until I hit the bone. Kate screamed. I grinned and began to cut down so slowly that it was almost like ripping the skin and flesh instead of cutting it clean.

"Wait, shall we have a little music?"

I walked over to the radio on my table and turned the radio to classical. I went back over to Kate and began. Kate screamed, and tears streamed down her face, but I didn't stop. I cut down the stomach, then down the sides like you would gut a fish. Kate was writhing and screaming, crying and bleeding.

"Your screams are so much better than this classical music, darling. Keep it up!"

I took hold of Kate's ribs, then, one by one I began to break them, each with a loud snap. Kate's voice soon turned hoarse, her screams dying a bit and sounding scratchy. She began to close her eyes, about to pass out.

"No, no, don't fall asleep on me now!" I slapped the side of her face trying to keep her awake but failed, so I took a syringe filled with adrenaline and injected some into Kate's bloodstream, making her jolt awake, and her blood began to gush. Before Kate could react, I yanked out her large intestine, making her screech out of pain.

"Oh, you can scream again!"

I quickly pulled out the small intestine, making Kate moan in pain. Then, suddenly and finally, her bowels emptied all over the floor like a shit stream in the sewers. Kate moaned, watching her dirty little life flash before her eyes.

I pulled up a chair in front of her, sat down, and watched her slowly die. But I did tell her a little story of how things would be so great with Laura and me, not to mention what I will do with Kate's body when she's finally dead. At that point, she began to spit blood. That was a normal process of dying slowly.

I took out my cell phone, turned on the camera application again, and flickered through the live feeds. Laura could be seen texting on her phone. Could she be texting Kate?

I laughed as I walked over to Kate and showed her, her best friend, Laura, on my cell phone,

"Say bye, bye,"

"You will N-never getaway W-with this!"

She was wrong. Now, if I play smart, I won't get caught. After a few minutes of watching Kate, her eyes began rolling to the back of her head. She died right in front of me. I waited an hour longer, just sitting there watching her lifeless body pouring out with the last bit of blood she had left. I'm not sure what I was waiting for, but I felt the excitement from this. Seeing Kate's body lifeless just felt like a victory.

I stood from where I was sitting and walked back upstairs and straight outside to the front porch. I walked around to the back of the cabin and went to the log shed. I stood there looking around.

"Perfect."

I picked up an old beaten shovel. Rusted to the point of no use, but it's all I had. I went back inside to get Kate's body prepared.

I rolled her up in my father's favourite shaggy white rug. It wasn't my kind of rug anyway. I dragged her up the stairs and out to the car and placed the shovel in the boot of my car along with Kate's body.

I was sat in the driver's seat looking through the camera feeds to find the love of my life having sex with the same person she'd fucked at the house party. I was angry. Betrayed. It was clear. I needed to dispose of him too, but I needed to be smart about this. I needed to stay focused on this present situation, and that was to dispose of Kate's body as soon as possible.

I switched on the engine, placed the gear in first, and took a right to the quiet road. Yet, I was paranoid that I might get stopped by the cops. The last thing I needed was to deal with them too. I took it easy while carefully watching my surroundings from my rear-view mirror, but I could see headlights and flashing police lights approaching fast. Sweat began pouring profusely, and my hands began to shake as well as my legs. ***Stay calm, stay calm.***

I couldn't outrun them, so I slowly pulled to the side of the road, but they sped past me as I stopped. The relief I felt was tremendous. It felt more like adrenalin racing through my veins rather than fear. Nonetheless, I continued my journey.

Arriving at the location, I turned off the engine to my car and stepped outside. I couldn't see anything... I underestimated the utter blackness of night-time in the woods. In my mind, the trees would be black trunks against a bluish charcoal sky, the path would become the deepest brown, and the moonlight would bleach the stones within it. Wasn't every painting of the woods at night been like that? Even if there were a moon tonight, its silvery rays would not penetrate the dense canopy above.

I turned on the headlights to give me some light. It could be no blacker in a coffin, six feet under and piled with dirt. I began to breathe the cool air. The darkness pressed in on me from all sides, and my body screamed for me to run. I walked to the boot of my car and opened it. I didn't look at Kate's body. I just took the shovel and began to dig her grave. The ground was soft and easy to dig. It took me only twenty-five minutes to dig three-foot. So, I dug six-foot. I walked back to the boot of my car and dragged her lifeless body over to her final resting place with her guts hanging out...

"You're not my problem anymore." I kicked her body into her new resting place and began to shovel the dirt back in. One down, many to go.

CHAPTER FOUR

I couldn't stop thinking about Laura while trying to get into a love film. I didn't have the concentration span for a stupid romantic comedy. I checked the camera app on my cell phone to see what Laura was up to. I scanned the feeds, and there she was, having a shower. I didn't overthink about her having sex with this guy. He's a dead man walking anyway. He was standing in her bedroom, putting on his pants. I wasn't planning on killing him on the same night as killing Kate, but I did want this over and done with, so I could make my move on Laura. I picked up my keys, went straight to my car, and drove to Laura's apartment again.

I saw the guy walking out of Laura's apartment two hours later. He reached in for a kiss; she accepted him. The truth is, it angered me. I felt the anger creeping through my body so fast that my fist tensed up, almost stopping the blood flow to my knuckles. Yet, the guy walked down the road, I wasn't sure how I was planning to kill him, but I turned on the engine to my car and started to follow him, carefully watching him as he walked away from Laura's apartment.

All I could feel at this very moment was rage. I pushed down hard on the acceleration, picking up more and more speed. I could see the bonnet of my car heading straight for him. I felt I had lost total control of my hands and feet.

I ramped up on the side of the sidewalk that he was on. I was unstoppable. I pushed even harder on the accelerator while screaming words never like before when the bonnet slammed into his back. He flew at least twenty yards, slamming to the ground like some test crash dummy. I stopped my car. I paused momentarily in shock. I got out to make sure he was dead.

I leaned down, checking him over. He looked dead to me, but then words slipped from my tongue,

"That's the last time you fuck my girl."

I was sure that I had killed him. I casually walked back to my car and headed straight back to my apartment to keep out of sight. I was in my apartment questioning myself repeatedly. What if I was seen? What if there were cameras? I started to Google the area on my cell phone. Lucky for me, they were no cameras installed in that area. A public member was catching the only thing I had to be worried about was my mug shot.

Yet, I had nothing more to do apart from sitting here watching Laura as she called someone on her cell.

"Kate, it's Laura. I'm getting really worried about you. You haven't responded to my last Text? Call me when you get this, please."

I laughed so hard, then placed my phone down on the coffee table and went into the kitchen to find something to eat. I was starving after this manic night. Mac and cheese were the only meal on the menu for me tonight. This was garbage food. I suppose I should be grateful to have something to digest if it digests.

After eating, I sat on the couch, overthinking again. How the hell did it come to this? Did I need to kill to be able to get closer to Laura?

I decided to stop thinking as I began to hit my low. It was wrong, and my behaviour was out of control, and I knew that. I was so angry that I started to hate myself even more after realizing what I had been doing. I went into the bedroom and underneath my bed was a box. I pulled it out and opened it. My father's handgun was resting inside. I picked it up and walked back into the living room. I couldn't take any more of this shit, I needed... No... I wanted to stop what I was thinking, but the only way to stop the thoughts was to press this **FUCKING GUN** to the side of my temple and pull the darn trigger! That's when I slowly placed the gun to my head and began to squeeze the trigger slowly. I was a few seconds away from blowing my brains out, but a thud at the door echoed throughout my apartment, followed by raised voices on the other side.

"THIS IS THE POLICE. OPEN THE DOOR, NOW!"

I had thoughts crossing my mind. Could they have found Kate's body, or was I seen running that guy down? I was tempted to end myself where I knelt. It's over. It's all over. But the thought of it was terrifying. I didn't have it in me. I did a few minutes ago, but now it is different. Yet, I placed the gun down on the ground and hid my phone inside my couch. I got up and slowly walked over to the door. All I could see from the window were flashing lights and torches dancing freely on my wall, lighting up the whole of my living room. I wasn't even dressed; I was only wearing grey joggers. Nonetheless, I slowly reached for the doorknob and turned it. I opened the door wide, and all I could hear was shouting while red dots were dancing around on my bare chest.

"LET ME SEE YOUR HANDS, NOW!"

The voices from the officers were muffled. I couldn't work out what the hell he was shouting. The officer's torches were blinding my view. I couldn't see anything.

"LET ME SEE YOUR HAND, NOW!" he went on.

The second time was clear as day. I didn't want to get shot, so I did exactly what he said,

"Okay, I'm doing it." I calmly say.

The officer worked fast. He started with my left arm, running his hands down from my shoulder to my wrist. He did the same with my right arm. He then searched me but found nothing.

"he's clean. No weapons," he says.

My eyes were drawn to the muzzle of the other officer's gun in front of me. It was still pointing at my chest. Nonetheless, I felt the cuffs were digging into both my wrists. He'd tightened them far more than he needed to. I complained, but it looked like he didn't give a shit. Yet, the officer escorted me to their patrol car while the other officer searched my apartment. He opened the side door to his police car and reached his hand flat on my head and shoved me in like I was nothing. I was pretty pissed off at that point. I knew I should have killed the guy a different way.

CHAPTER FIVE

Three years later. I was locked up in a high-maximum prison. Ask me where I was. I couldn't tell you. It was easy being locked up for the first few months, but it got frustrating by the minute as time took its toll. The cops still didn't know I had killed Kate, but the guy I mowed down... what's his name again... That's it, his name was Carl. Yeah, that guy died. I thought he would make it, but he died halfway through my trial. I have just two years left or one year on good behaviour if I'm lucky. Put it this way; I'm not finished. Laura will always be the love of my life, and right now, I need her the most. I felt the devil was out to get me in here; I can feel its dark shadow peeking over my shoulders every darn day. Nonetheless, I'm sitting inside my cell, trying to keep away from the rest of the prison population.

These people are the devil's followers, and the last thing I need is an extended prison sentence for getting into a fight. Yet, I hear the young ones crying themselves to sleep; many kill themselves after day three, not that I blame them for killing themselves... I would, too, if I was here for life. An old convict called Jason whom I get on well with said to me with outflung arms that embraced the entire upper yard,

"Son, a prison yard is a microcosm of society at large. What you see here is a miniature replica of the entire world."

As I followed his gaze to that windblown, rain-battered patch of asphalt, pigeons, and galls, I struggled to make sense of his statement. It was hard to see the analogies to the free world. Convicts in raincoats played dominoes while rain ran off their hats. A beady-eyed gun-rail guard stood above them with a 30-30 rifle in his hand, watching every prisoner.

After seeing many years and prison yards go by, I've found his words hold a lot of truth. In ways, I have regret for my crimes, but you can't go back to what was done, and that bothers me a lot. We have our economy in prisons. Cigarettes were a hundred cents a pack. Sandwiches were a pack. A pack would get a shirt, or a pair of pants pressed, or "Bonorooed," as we call it. A quart of prison wine, or "pruno," cost five packs and fifty percent interest on loans. Most of those prices are still the same, though cigarettes are four dollars a pack these days.

Another actual price increase has been on hard drugs, and that's entirely understandable. Today, the cocaine business is a much more dirty and more dangerous occupation than five years ago. The demand has gradually surpassed the supply. We have our gang members, serial killers, conmen, factory workers, religious groups, wine shops, grocery stores, lenders, laundries, artists, musicians, intellectuals, and people of all political persuasions. You name it; we've got it. We've got the whole world in our can. Sad, but the way you look at it, the more it becomes a reality.

Yet, prison restores order and certainty in a person's life. Meals are served according to a rigid schedule; laundry is exchanged at definite times; sick calls, mail calls, and visits are all at fixed hours on designated days. We are accustomed to breakfast at five and lunch at one o'clock, supper at seven. McDonald's is only a dim memory. Sometimes I wonder if I would ever see a McDonald's again...

Yet, in prison, we are confronted with another certainty, a job. Everyone in prison works unless physically or mentally unable to do so. The employment ranges from factories to janitorial, kitchen, laundry, and maintenance crews. Everything is scheduled.

A convict can also get marijuana, a shot of dope, or a drink of booze now and then. Not enough for a habit, but enough to take the edge off things. Sometimes I felt I needed all of those just to get by, but I'm doing OK... so far.

That reminds me... a new mental patient here not long ago walked into a cell-block office where a guard was sitting and began cutting the officer in the head with a single-edge razor blade. I know, right? Crazy guy! Yet, they never exchanged a word. It took a multitude of stitches to close the wound.

As a result of that incident, we are all treated like people with mental health conditions instead of actual convicts. Most regular officers aren't sure whether we are here because of insanity or criminality. They can't afford any chances in a cell block with only one guard and two hundred convicts. This attitude breeds distrust and poor communication between staff and convicts.

I sure have learned a lot from being here. One day I dream of saying goodbye to this nasty place and living a life with Laura. We understand that the most important thing is our set routine in the prison setting—something we do every day. Our routine is the motor that drives us over the hump of time. We fine-tune it and get it down to a science. We are confined to one cell block and not allowed in any other. We can go to the yard, the mess hall, or our job from our cell block.

Nonetheless, it's one in the afternoon here, almost lunchtime. I was sitting inside my cell, cage if you will; I suppose it looks more like a cage rather than a cell.

You get three walls, a toilet, a sink, and a sliding door with bars. I walked outside my cell, leaning over the railings and looking down on all the convicts. Some days I couldn't believe I was here, but I was. Yet, I went back inside my cell and sat on my bed reading a book. I hate books, but it's not like I had anything better to do with my life right now.

Yet, still lying here with my pillows pressed against the wall and my book in my hands, I could hear single hollow footsteps walking towards my cell. I kept reading while trying to block out the annoying dangling keys and hollow footsteps. It got closer towards my cell, but then a deep voice emerged,

"Anthony, visitor. Let's move." he firmly goes on.

I was shocked. Who the hell would want to visit me? I stood and placed the book firmly on my bed and followed the prison officer through the prison into the courtyard to the visiting area. I was standing by the visiting room door when the officer said,

"No funny stuff, got it?"

"Relax," I replied.

The officer opened the door and waved me inside. A man sat before me smoking a cigarette while holding a notepad and pen. He says,

"Take a seat."

He was a middle-aged guy, a rough-looking chap with a slight stubble facial hair, looks like a cop... smells like one. I took a seat. I was waiting for him to do me for Kate's murder. Why else would he be sitting before me with an evil look on his face? Looking at him where I sat, it felt as if I knew everything about him. The cheap suit smells badly of cigars like he smoked more than a twenty-pack a day. He had no wife, and he didn't look like the father type. He was in bad shape too.

"What can I do for you, officer?"

"It's more of what I can do for you. And it's detective."

I was intrigued by what he was about to say to me,

"Go on," I replied, carefully listening to what he had to say,

"I want to offer you an early release, but you have to do something for me in return."

I felt he wanted me to do something huge, but I couldn't work out what it was.

"I have a prisoner coming in today, he is still on trial, and the trial could last a long time, years maybe, but if I get a fake witness saying he confessed everything, then he would be locked up for sooner, and everyone is happy, what do you think?"

I didn't know what to think or say, only this would grant me an early release. There had to be more to this.

"Well... I know what they do to lags in here, and it isn't pleasant. One guy got slashed. I leaned forward and whispered. One guy even got raped."

But I knew I couldn't say no, I would get released, and I'll see Laura sooner! He handed me a document and said,

"All you must do is practice what you have to say on the trial for him to get convicted and for you to go home on that very same day. You will never have to see this place again."

The document he handed was everything I needed to memorize for the trial. I have a good memory, so this is nothing!

"And you can promise me that I will be released?" I asked, curious about why he had chosen me for this.

He pushed another document over to me and said,

"Sign here. This guarantees that you will be released once he is convicted."

I sat here reading what the guy had done. He killed his family with a chainsaw—nasty bastard.

I know I'm no better, but I believe that killing your own family is against everything. I then said,

"I'll do it,"

"He is called Hope. Wing D-12, cell 15. That's your cell."

I signed the document and placed the script down my pants. I was then escorted back to my cell. After all that was said and done, I sat patiently waiting for this, Hope guy. What kind of name is Hope?

Nonetheless, all I had to do was spend a few days talking to him, so it looked like we were talking. *Easy.* I suppose I was curious why this guy, Hope, killed his family. Maybe he'll confess to it, or perhaps he would be so desperate to keep his mouth shut? I know I would be.

Four hours later, I was shaving over the sink in my cell. My name was then called,

"Anthony, you have a new cellmate."

I turned around, suddenly, stumbling back in shock. That guy, Hope, was one big guy, I tell you. He was covered in tattoos across his face, arms, and chest. He was around six-foot, with a heavy build. I wouldn't want to piss him off in a dark alleyway. I only needed to wait three days for the trial. Oh, boy, I am counting down to that day.

I looked at him for a moment longer and swallowed hard. After the prison officer left, Hope returned a stern gaze. I didn't want to get in his way, so I went to the courtyard.

I was sitting in the courtyard, getting some air into my lungs while thinking about the trial, but Hope took the chair beside me and asked for a cigarette. I hand him one. He lights it, leans back, and lets out a sigh that sounds like a truck tire going flat.

Oh no, I think to myself, here it comes! Sure enough, he begins talking. The courts trampled on his rights. His lawyer sold him out by the sounds of it. Maybe his wife was doing him wrong that he killed her. On and on, he goes for half an hour and never mentions any crime he committed. I was hoping he would spill out his crimes. I rise in the middle of his monolog—it's one I've heard thousands of times in places like this. I then say,

"Well, buddy, I'm tired, and I'm going to bed. Tomorrow, I'll get up and do the same thing all over again."

He laughed as I walk back to my cell.

CHAPTER SIX

I could hear the rain was still heavy outside. I spent most of the day practicing my words in the hole. I was moved here because of the trial tomorrow; soon, all this will be over. It wasn't pleasant in the hole at all, and it smelt like piss and shit, it almost felt like I was sleeping in a public toilet, but at least it had a bed. Everyone locked up in the hole was shouting abuse to the officers. They would go on for hours just throwing vile abuse at the officers. At one point, I called back at them to tell them to shut the fuck up. It was driving me crazy. However, I am crazy in some sense. There wasn't much more I could do apart from repeatedly reading this document. I must have read my lines a thousand times, but I turned over and went to sleep as boredom took its toll.

The next day, the day I had been waiting for. It felt like years until the trial. I got up and began pacing up and down impatiently while practicing what I needed to say to the judge. I couldn't wait for that key to unlock the door to my cell. I could feel the butterflies in my stomach. I got dressed in a black suit given to me last night by one of the officers. I spent at least three hours or more talking to him last night. Nice guy. I could hear an officer's footsteps echoing through the cold, dampened corridor. I took a deep breath as the door began to unlock. I was nervous. It was time.

"Anthony, let's move."

I was escorted to the prison van. The officer checked my restraints and placed me in the back of the truck, but as he was about to shut the doors, he said,

"Get it right, and you get to leave this shithole."

Yet, I didn't spend much time with this Hope guy, and there was nothing I learned from him either, only that he killed his family, and I was to make sure he stayed behind bars for the rest of his life. I was nervous but calm. We had been travelling for a while when the van came to a complete halt. I couldn't see where we was because they were no windows, but suddenly the door opened. The detective I made a deal with stands before me with a big grin on his face. I hope he wasn't planning on keeping me behind bars.

"Let's go, Anthony," he said.

I stepped out of the van and looked up at the morning sun. It was beautiful as can be. After all these years of being locked up in a high maximum, I was thankful for this. Yeah, I got to see the sun, but not like this. I looked around, seeing people going about their day. They will never see or feel what I do.

"Let's move." an officer says.

I was escorted into the courthouse and placed in a room with the detective.

He said this would be simple enough and nothing could go wrong unless I slipped up and strayed away from my lines. We spoke briefly before we were called into the courtroom.

"You will be fine, Anthony."

I was out of my restraints and escorted to the courtroom, where I would give my statement to the jury. I was nervous, but the worst that could happen was I finished off the rest of my sentence with this, Hope guy and became his bitch. I still don't understand why his mother called him Hope.

Nonetheless, the double doors ahead of me opened wide, and three judges sat before me. I swallowed hard as I made my way down to the dock. Everyone's eyes fixed on me, making me feel uneasy if you know what I mean? I made my way up to the dock and sat down while gazing around the courtroom. My eyes caught a bible just resting in front of me on the panel. I have so many sins already, so swearing on this would be easy. The three judges stood and firmly shouted,

"ALL RISE."

We all stood and then were told to sit. That's when I was told to swear on the bible. I did what they asked by placing my right hand on top of the Bible but was then asked to give my statement right after. I froze, suddenly looking around the room. Yet, I was severely sweating at that point.

"Anthony, we need your statement, please," the judge says.

"Yeah, sorry, I'm just really nervous; so many people."

The judge politely nods his head.

I didn't want to be here any longer, so that's when I lied and told them what the detective wished me to say. It wasn't as bad as I thought it would be. After a while, my nervousness became too calm, and I quickly told my side of the story, even if it was a lie.

"That will be all." the judge remarks.

I was then escorted back to the interview room, where the detective would wait. As time went on, the detective came walking back into the room,

"You did it," he says, with a grin. He was excited.

"So, what now?" I replied, curious about what was going to happen to me next.

"Anthony, as promised, you are a free man."

I could not even speak. I felt my heart skip a beat, and butterflies began to turn in my stomach.

Am I free? The only person I could think of was Laura. I grabbed my stuff and headed for the exit. I walked outside, looking around. No officers holding my arms. No guns pointing at my chest. I was a free man once again. I stood still and went into my last thoughts on that hell hole. No matter how we approach the issue intellectually, it doesn't dampen the rage we acquire from being packed in gloomy cages while there are blue sky and sunshine just beyond the wall. We had to share that place down to our germs. If one gets the flu, we'd all get it. When our routines were disrupted, chaos was once again among us. The future seemed fragmented and uncertain. Should our keepers choose to deal with pain, chaos, and destruction, a strange resolve takes hold among the convicts. Not me; I'm a free man now.

CHAPTER SEVEN

Ask me where my home is these days... I would struggle to find an answer. Everything I did for Laura seemed for nothing. After coming out of prison, I lost almost everything; thankfully, I had my cabin to go back to, if nothing. Laura had moved away from her old apartment. Everything felt different. Yet, I was sitting in the basement of my cabin, crying. I was beaten up about it. The thought of her being out there alone cut so deep.

I needed to find her; I was getting desperate by the minute. But I did know where to begin my first search. One idea struck my mind. I knew her full name. I started my search on Facebook, but after a while, no results matched. It's like she just vanished off the face of the earth. It was like looking for a needle in a haystack. I guess the only way I will find out is from her old landlord. I looked up Laura's old address on my new cell phone to find a contact number for her old landlord. My new cell phone was secondhand, nothing special at all.

After searching for hours on the internet, I did find a number. I wrote it down and started punching in the numbers on my cell phone. That's when it rang and rang until finally a middle-aged lady answered the phone and said,

"Hello?"

"Hi, I'm trying to track down an old tenant of yours?"

"I'm sorry, but I'm not allowed to give out any tenants' personal information,"

"She's my sister, and I lost her contact information. It would mean so much to me; see, her mother is dying."

Sad, I know, but how else can I convince her to hand over a bloody contact number?

"Oh my, that's terrible news, and I am truly sorry. What's the tenant's name?" she asks.

"Her name is Laura Edwards."

After I had mentioned her name, the lady had gone silent for a moment longer, but she then said,

"Ah, she moved to Texas, Houston, I think? It was a year ago now. Some new job, she said. One second, I think I still have her new number somewhere, see, she still owes me a little rent if you can remind her?"

"Sure. No problem."

After hearing she had moved to Huston, my heart felt like it would stop.

"Here we go. Do you have a pen and paper to hand?"

"Fire away."

I noted her number and hung up. I then punched in the numbers to Laura's cell phone. It rang. I was desperate to hear her voice. That's when her cell phone answered,

"Hello, Laura speaking?"

I didn't speak. I just needed to hear her voice. I missed her so badly!

"Okay, whoever you are, you need to stop calling me." she firmly went on.

She then hung up the phone. I needed to get over to Texas for a few days to begin my search. I can't let her slip away from me again. I packed a few things in my bag and phoned a cab to take me to the airport.

I sat down while waiting for a cab and began to think of a few things. From the minute I saw her... the first time... she was jogging. I haven't been able to think of anything else, anyone else. She had taken

over my whole world, my whole life. I think about her all the time, every day. I remember everything she said, every single word, even if they were bad words. Sometimes I felt I was out of my depth as I passionately, obsessively told myself how much I loved her. I tried to understand my emotions, and I wanted to know why I killed someone over her. It's not a good feeling to acknowledge this, but I take tremendous comfort in the fact that I've done all wrong, and it cannot be undone. It's a liberating and exhilarating sensation when you realize that you've done everything in your hands to achieve something, reach somewhere, and beyond these things are not in your control... well, that's how I felt anyway.

The cab had sounded its horn. I picked up my bag, keys, and phone and I walked towards the cab and opened the door when the driver said,

"I don't have much of a playlist for this journey, so you will have to make do with the radio,"

"I'm only going to the airport."

I got in the back just keeping myself to myself. I wasn't up for some chit-chat with some random cab driver. I just wanted to get to the airport and get over to Texas as soon as possible. Yet, I was sitting here as the driver drove me to the airport; I was alternating between screaming and crying. It took a few minutes to realize tears were streaming down my face. I thought I was all cried out over her. The driver looks back at me through the mirror, "Say, you OK back there?"

I felt frustrated. I screamed, and kicked the back seats, scratching my face like an alley cat backed into a corner. The cab driver stopped the car on the side of the highway and got out and reached for his cell phone. I tried desperately to get out to stop him from calling the cops. I was trapped. I got angrier, so I repeatedly kicked in the window. The window shattered into millions of pieces.

I climbed out and began to walk towards him. Yet, I looked like death. He took a few steps back onto the busy highway. I slowly looked to my right, seeing an oncoming lorry, he stepped back again, and the lorry took him, causing the lorry driver to sway from left to right. I was smiling as I knew what was about to happen. I could then see the cab driver flying into midair. ***Just my fucking luck!*** I acted quickly and looked in the driver's seat of the cab, hoping he'd left the keys in the ignition, and he did. I didn't wait around; I just got in and sped off. I knew the cab driver's accident wasn't by my hands, but the situation probably made my life a lot worse. In a way, I was responsible.

I was driving along the busy highway and thinking about many things. I felt like my mind was being hijacked like it was trying to replace my soul with some demon. Yet, the saying goes, if your life is as messed up as it seems, then it's repairable if you embrace every moment. Strange... sounds more like a falsification if you ask me.

Yet, still driving along the highway, I began to see signs for the airport. I was relieved to see the signposts. It was fifty-five miles away. This is going to be a long drive.

CHAPTER EIGHT

I never thought I would get a second chance to make things right. Arriving in Huston, I checked into a motel until the morning. They were nothing I could do right now, and I was pretty much tired, hungry, and grumpy from the long-winded journey. I sat on the bed in my motel room, looking around. Nothing special. A floor, a door, a window, a bed, a television, and a bathroom. I stayed in some better places and many far worse ones too. That being said... the jail was the worse one. The walls of the motel were thin. I could hear the sounds coming from the room next door. Not enough to recognize words, but certainly raised voices. Did it sound like a man arguing with his girlfriend? I stood from sitting on my bed and grabbed a cold coke from the vending machine. I could hear the shouting more clearly as the vending machine was between theirs and mine.

Yet, still standing there while necking down the cold coke in the pissing hard rain. The door suddenly opened. A man walked out, slamming the door behind him and gently rested his back against the door, and said,

"Don't women just drive you fucking crazy?"

I didn't know what to say to that. I just laughed with a slight shoulder shrug. I didn't want to be caught up in someone's arguments. I had problems of my own.

Nonetheless, he reached deep into his pocket and took out a cigarette packet. He lit his cigarette and said,

"You smoke?"

I hesitated for a moment.

"Why not." I laughed.

He passed me a cigarette, and we just stood there talking about his problems for at least an hour. Boring! But the guy seriously had lady issues. Yet, I couldn't be bothered to listen to his issues any longer, so I cut him off and said,

"I'm sure things will work out for you both, buddy. Anyway, I must get back inside and get some rest; been a long flight. Take care now,"

"You too, buddy."

I went back inside, switched on the TV, and rested on the bed, but I suddenly heard a massive bang coming from the room next to me. *Why can't people relax?* I got out of bed and walked to the window to see the man from next door throwing his bags in the boot of his car while still shouting abuse at his girlfriend, that remained inside the motel room,

"YOU KNOW WHAT... WE ARE OVER. IM DONE WITH YOU BITCH!" he went on.

He wasn't kidding either. He got in his car and left her in the motel room independently. It wasn't any of my business. I got back into bed, thanking the lord above for the silence. I switched off the box set and began to relax, but I couldn't sleep. I rolled over to check the alarm clock on the bedside table. It was three in the morning, and I heard crying faintly from the room next door. I hesitated but couldn't allow someone to cry all night, especially when trying to sleep. I got out of bed and opened my door. I stepped outside and knocked on the door.

"J-Just a minute P-please," she says, as her voice crackled with emotions. She opened her door and looked right at me. I wasn't expecting this. The one and only Laura Edwards were standing right before my eyes. I was static! I couldn't believe it. Nonetheless, she tried to speak, but she could barely utter her words. I played it cool and said,

"You're that girl from the party many years back, right? You told me to have a mental health weekend?" She smiled and said,

"I gave you such a hard time, didn't I?"

"Don't worry about it. Anyhow, that was a long time ago. Why are you crying... and why are you on your own?" I replied, making out I didn't know a thing.

She invited me inside. Hell, yeah, I took her offer. This just opened a whole lot of doors for me. I went inside, shutting the door behind me. She took a seat at the end of her bed and broke down in tears. She was still as beautiful as ever.

I couldn't stand there and watch her cry any longer. I slowly coated towards her and sat next to her. She then rests her head on my shoulder and says,

"I have been through hell and back. My best mate, Kate, went missing years ago, and my ex-boyfriend got knocked over by a car. And now my recent boyfriend walks out on me? I just don't get it?"

"Well, he couldn't have loved you that much to walk out on you," I replied, totally avoiding what she was saying about her friend, Kate. The mention of Kate brings a chill to my spine! Yet, Laura looked up into my eyes as I got lost in hers for at least a minute before she reached in for a kiss.

My heart felt like it had stopped beating. This was it. She pulls in closer, her soft lips inches away from mine. I needed her so fucking bad that I gave into her sudden demand. Yet, I couldn't help but think about the guy that just walked out on her. *What if he comes back? What if he wants her back? Would she jump for him?* It was clear. I knew I had to kill him to make my final move on Laura. Me sitting here was fate, not luck.

Yet, Laura and I were making out when I suddenly pulled away and said,

"Maybe this is a little too soon?"

"Oh my god... I am so sorry," a note to surprise in her voice.

"It's fine. Maybe I can invite you over to my place for dinner sometime?"

She stops and wonders in thoughts and says,

"You know what, that would be so great." she smiled. I knew what game I was playing, and exactly how it should be played down.

CHAPTER NINE

I couldn't believe my luck when I saw Laura at the motel, and here I was, thinking I would never get to see her again. We started talking and kissing for most of the night. I felt we got on rather well. I gave her clear signs that I was really into her, but my problem was that she had only just broken up with someone. Nonetheless, I was back home, the only home I had left after coming out of jail. It's a nice place, and it had that cozy touch.

Yet, the wood was crackling away in the fire while the sound of the wind pressed against each window of the cabin; it had that sense of calm. I was expecting Laura over for dinner, I'm not a great cook, and I didn't know what I would cook, but Google is my best friend. After searching Google nothing looked easy, and it wasn't going to be very long until she was here. I guess I'm going for the steak and chips.

I placed the steak into the pan on low and went down into the basement to check on her ex-boyfriend, Jack. Ha-ha, Yeah, I didn't kill him just yet. I have so much to tell him before I do kill him. I want him to suffer. I want him to hear how well Laura and I will get on. The poor guy was hung by his arms from the basement ceiling. I walked down just as he was about to escape the chains that held him, prisoner. Sneaky little shit!

"And where do you think you're going, Jack?"

"YOU ARE FUCKING CRAZY. he shouts. I secured the chains so he couldn't ruin my night with Laura.

"Don't worry; I will tell you how well everything goes with Laura and me tonight after I fuck her brains out."

I could see the pain in his eyes as tears dropped to the cold stone ground beneath his cheek. Desperate pleas fall on deaf ears. However, nobody was there to help him, and he knew that. Yet, I walked over to the table across the basement and saw a whip. I picked it up and began to whip him so bad. Why whip him? Why not! It was fun.

"N-No... S-Stop, p-please... J-Just stop," his raspy voice begs.

"Why did it have to be me? Why couldn't it have been somebody else," he cries.

"You're the ex, buddy, and what a shellfish thing to say."

I whipped even harder, making him bleed.

"Augh!" he cries out in agony once the whip slams into his back. He was desperately gasping for the breath that was forced out of his lungs. A burning feeling danced up and down his back.

"Please, just stop,"

"Come on; don't lose consciousness on me now! I was just starting to have fun!"

I placed the whip back onto the table and picked up a surgical knife and walked back over to him, and said,

"I'm afraid I have no choice but to cut out your voice box... can't have you shouting your mouth off while Laura's here, can we?"

I pressed the knife to his throat and cut out his voice box, I didn't mind the blood at all. His eyes were rolling to the back of his head while his blood was just pissing out like a fountain. I laughed. I walked back upstairs and locked the basement door behind me. He won't die. Well, he might do.

An hour later, the doorbell rang. I was nervous like hell. I walked over to the door while checking how I looked in the mirror that was just by the door. Not bad, not bad at all. I opened the door, and Laura stood before me, looking like a million dollars. She was beautiful, but it was the same outfit she wore when I first met her at that house party. Not that I had a problem with that... It brings back bad memories, but I'm sure I can look past that. She held up a carry bag and said,

"I bought some beers for us to get this party started."

My world was about to change. And I knew it was just a matter of time before it did.

CHAPTER TEN

The relentless downpour was pouring down hard outside, which began at dusk. It's been a week talking with Laura, and she is impressive. Laura had stayed over that night, and she had never left my side since. I think we got on rather well. Yeah, we hit off wrong, but after getting to know each other, I feel she understood me, as I understood her. It was hard having her here because of her ex-boyfriend's body living in my basement. Thinking of that, I will have to get rid of him very soon.

Nonetheless, I went to sleep next to Laura with the sound of the rain drumming on the slate roof of the cabin. I drifted off into a calm state. I began dreaming. The dream went from good to bad. I dreamed of Kate waking from her grave and knocking on my door... not a nice feeling. Can you imagine the chances of that happening? Slim, I know, but it would be terrifying for sure.

The following day, I rolled to my side and glanced at my alarm clock; 5:00 am. Who gets up at such a time in the morning? Not me! But it was nice being woke to the smell of freshly cooked bacon and eggs. I got out of bed and walked over to the window to open the blinds when I heard Laura say,

"Shit. This has never happened to me before!"

At that moment I thought she had seen her ex in the basement. I ran out of the bedroom and down the stairs into the kitchen and said,

"Are you OK? What's wrong?" a note to surprise in my voice.

"Well... I was trying to make fresh eggs but turned into complete shit."

She laughs while holding the egg tosser in one hand while her other hand is on her hip. She was so darn hot. She was wearing a pair of grey hot pants and what seemed to be... one of my shirts? Now, this was a big deal, in a good way, of course.

"I think those eggs are outdated anyway. I thought they were fresh," I reply.

"WHAT!" a note to surprise in her voice.

"I've been far too busy to think about shopping... I was planning to shop, but I got distracted, see?"

"One second." she replied.

She rushed upstairs, and a few moments later, she picked up her phone, purse, and car key and walked to the front door,

"You are leaving over bad eggs?" I ask.

I stood from sitting on the couch and walked towards her.

"I'm going shopping; we need food... badly."

She had reassured me by kissing me on the cheek. I walked her to the door and waited by the front door until she had left so I could get rid of her ex... somehow?

As Laura was about to drive away, she shouted out her car window,

"We need wood, so start chopping!"

Oh, I will, I will indeed.

"Okay," I reply.

Thoughts crossed my mind on how I could get rid of her ex's body. Burn him out the back? *Perfect*.

Yet, I watched her pull out onto the quiet road, and she sped off. I shut the door, locking it behind me, and went straight down to the basement.

I walked deeper into the cold but damp basement to find her ex was missing.

Oh shit. I thought he was dead?

"Oh, Laura's ex, where are you hiding?"

I stood listening for any sudden movements. That's when I heard the basement door slam shut. I stood in no rush at all. I lit up my first smoke of the day and took a deep drag, cracking my neck. I was going to finish this fucker. Yet, I was a victim of my own mind. I threw down my smoke and began chasing after this Lab rat.

"STOP FOOLING AROUND," I shout.

Yet, I walked up the stairs and opened the door, and there he was, he was right there waiting for me holding a nine-inch kitchen knife. He looked petrified. His hands could be seen dancing, and his legs could be seen shaking. He also couldn't say shit to me after I had taken out his voice box.

"Why don't we sit down and chat about this? You can use a pen and paper, and I can use my voice?" I sarcastically say.

I slowly coated towards him, but he put out a nice stiff left which he planned to follow with a right cross. I slipped to the left, which threw him off enough so that I could step inside the right cross and get a handful of his hair. I pulled his head forward and broke his nose with my head. Still holding his hair in one hand, I got my other hand into his crotch, put my shoulder into him, lifted him off the ground, and slammed him down on the kitchen side. He grunted and went limp. When I stood back, he slowly slid off the kitchen side. I couldn't wait a moment longer, so I picked up the knife and slowly sliced through his throat like he was my Christmas turkey. That was the end of him. I needed to get rid of his body as soon as possible, but it would be impossible to get rid of it right now.

Yet, I looked out the kitchen window, and the log shed was my best bet until Laura went out again. I wrapped his body in cling film, mopped up the blood, and then dragged him to the front door. I went outside to check that no one was around. After looking around, I dragged his body out the front and straight to the log shed. But as I was dragging him into the log shed, I heard a car pull up. *Fuck sake, not now!* I covered him over with a blue plastic sheet and locked the shed door behind me. That's when I made my way back to the front of the cabin, holding some firewood. That's when I saw Laura.

"Slacking a little, aren't you?"

"No, I was just doing a few jobs around the cabin,"

"Oh really, like what?" she sarcastically replies.

"You caught me red-handed, Laura."

She laughs while holding the sexiest but most forceful gaze. Maybe this is it for us? After everything, I have done to be with her. I do think I did what was best. I guess killing was the only way to be with her. I just pray it stays this way so I don't have to kill anymore. Sometimes I go over my thoughts and ask myself why I kill. never seem to find the answers; I just keep doing what I feel is best.

CHAPTER ELEVEN

She loves me, she loves me not, she loves me, she loves me not, she loves me, she loves me **NOT!** I thought she was the love of my life. I trusted her, but it seemed I trusted an evil twisted **BITCH!** How can I ever learn to trust her again? We spent most of the night talking for hours to find she was texting her ex that whole time, even though he was dead. The fact that she texted him saying she still loved him pissed me off. I confronted her about this, but she said she was being silly; I didn't believe her. I did everything for her. We went Downtown for a night out, even took her for dinner, then we went to see a movie. We hit off tremendously, and things were moving smoothly as they should. We made love repeatedly. I can't forget how nice it felt as our skin touched.

Yes, it was passionate, but now it seems unreal. It looks like it was for nothing.

Yet, I'm thinking of ways to get her to love me and not this dead guy in my log shed. Sometimes it feels almost impossible. Nonetheless, Laura left for a few days. She said something about her father passing away. Obviously, I didn't want to intrude... I know she will be back. That reminds me; it gives me time to get rid of Laura's beloved ex's outback. I didn't want him buried; I decided to chop him up and dissolve his body in acid.

Yet, I grabbed my coat, stepped outside, and looked up into the night skies. It was a beautiful sight, but It was freezing and snowy. The snow was up to my knees. This was winter snow, after all. I struggled to get to the log shed, but I finally made it after a few minutes of battling the snow. I unlocked the door and stepped inside, locking it behind me. I gazed around the shed looking for my axe, but my eyes rested the longest on the tree grinder just by the body; this would be better than chopping him up and dissolving him in acid, which would take hours. I walked over to the grinder and checked it over.

I was hoping the darn thing still works. I plugged it in to see if it still worked after sitting there for at least seventeen years.

I pressed the little green button on the side, and it failed to work.

I guess acid is the best way. I dragged his body back inside the cabin and into the bathroom. The guy was heavy enough.

Nonetheless, I picked him up and threw him into the bathtub. I went down to the basement to get two bottles of acid. My father kept it for disposing of the dead animals he'd hunted back then. ***It must be fate***. I picked up the two acid bottles and went upstairs and into the bathroom. It was now or never.

I covered my mouth with a mask and began to pour both acid bottles all over his lifeless body. After a few minutes, I began to gag badly; the smell was intense that I wished the grinder worked, but I guess the acid was working. While waiting for his body to dissolve into goo, I gave Laura a text.

"Hey, Laura, I hope things are OK for you; I can't wait to speak with you over the phone tomorrow."

The only message I got back was, ok, Speak soon.

I suppose that was better than receiving no messages at all. Yet, after waiting an hour, there was no ex left to dissolve; I was relieved to see it worked.

I cleaned up all the mess I left behind and covered all my tracks. After that, I casually sat in front of the fire, loading it up with more wood to warm up the cabin.

The cold swept through the cabin so fast that my bones felt like they would cease. Yet, hours seemed to pass quickly, and not even a text from Laura to say goodnight, but I suppose she has a lot on her mind. I decided to call it a night and sleep on the couch.

The morning proved to be the coldest yet. I didn't even want to move because I knew I would feel the cold even worse when I moved. The fire was dying out but could quickly be revived could just get the courage to move my ass. I sat up and quickly leaped over to the fireplace and threw a couple more logs in. After a few minutes, I had a perfect working fire again.

I looked straight at my cell phone on the floor as it rang. Laura's name could be seen flashing up. I bent down and picked it up. I then answered my cell phone.

"Hey, Laura, are you OK?" a note to surprise in my voice.

"Hi, Anthony, yeah, I'm OK; I just thought I would give you a call and let you know I'll be back this evening if you still want me?"

I was static at this point. I missed her like crazy! Yet, I felt selfish.

"It's not too soon, though, right?"

"No, I just really need you right now."

Hearing that made me feel alive again. I guess I was the only person she had left right now. Her mother passed away three years ago. She has no siblings, cousins, aunts, granddads, or nans. The poor girl is basically on her own.

"That's fine. Well, I'm right here for when you get back,"

"Thank you, Anthony. Right, I will see you later tonight, I got a few things to take care of, and I will make my way back soon.",

She hung up, leaving me thinking about the good things we had yet to come. Maybe she was just being silly when she texted her ex? She deleted his number right in front of me and said I'm the one she wanted to be with. Nonetheless, I spent most of my day cleaning and airing the cabin from the smell of her ex's in the draining system.

Yet, I was in the kitchen washing up the pots and just trying to live an everyday life and putting the killing behind me, but I swore I saw something moving in the backyard just by the log shed. I looked closer but couldn't see because of the snow blinded my view. As I looked harder, it looked more like a woman?.it looked like... Kate? I casually walked to the front door and opened it.

"YOU WILL NEVER GET AWAY WITH THIS!"

I stood almost paralyzed by what I had seen, but she vanished right before me. *It was Kate. It's impossible?* I knew this was my mind playing tricks, so I shut the door and sat down in the living room with the music on full.

Nonetheless, a week ago, I managed to get my car back from the compound with minor damage to the bonnet. But I can't use it until I dig it out of the snow. Luckily for me, the road gritters had been to fill up the grit box just by the entrance to my driveway. I needed to get some groceries for when Laura gets back; it gets me away from here for a while. I grabbed my keys and coat and headed outside to free my car from the deep snow. I stood there and took one look.

Ah, man, this isn't going to be easy.

CHAPTER TWELVE

I t took me half an hour to get my car out of the snow. But in the end, I did it with a lot of effort. I had to renew my tax and insurance before I got any groceries. I was almost out of pocket after working out my bills. I had no job, no mortgage, and no income at all. I was living off $1,000. I decided to head to the bank to open a loan account until I could find a stable job. I drove through Downtown at the busiest time of the day. It was 10:30 am. Yet, still moving along the busy roads, I saw a bank.

I pulled to the side of the road, switched off the engine, checked I had documents, and got out, stretching my arms. It was good to be away from that cabin, even for a few hours or more.

Nonetheless, I walked towards the bank and through the double doors.

It was busy.

Yet, I waited in the long cue while the idiot in front decided to argue with the cashier about his empty bank account. Well, maybe he should have been more careful with his cash. You get those that get a wage and go out drinking without thinking of the bill the next day.

Nonetheless, he got escorted out of the building, and the queue got smaller and smaller until it was my turn.

"Hi, I would like to open a loan account with you today, please?"

"That's no problem at all, sir. If you could just take a seat, I will get someone right to you; in the meantime, please take this form and fill out all the questions while you're waiting, please."

I took the form and sat down. I took one look at the form and didn't know where to start, so I started with my address and all that critical stuff needed for an account.

Ten minutes later, a lady came over to me and said,

"Are you the gentleman that needs a loan account today?"

"Yes, that would be me,"

"If you would please follow me." She smiles.

I stood from where I was sitting and followed her towards a small room, but, as I was following her, three armed men came storming through the main doors firing their weapons into the air and shouting,

"EVERYONE ON THE GROUND, NOW!"

Cries and screams filled the air as one security guard was shot in the back. I pushed the lady into the room and shut the door behind us. The young lady was kneeling behind a filing cabinet, texting on her phone.

"Hey, lady... not a time to be checking your Instagram." I sarcastically say.

All I wanted was a stupid loan, some money to see me through!

Nonetheless, the armed men were shouting at everyone to hand over any cell phone devices, or they would be shot without warning. I wasn't planning on playing hero, but I was looking for a way out of this bank. I wasn't thinking about anyone else.

"Is there any way out of here?" I whispered.

She whispers back, "No, only the fire exit behind the cashier's desk." she points.

"WHAT, YOU DON'T HAVE ONE FOR THE PUBLIC?" I slightly raised my voice.

The look on her face was a clear sign that this was the only way out.

There was no way of getting to the exit while the armed men watched the only exit. I decided to wait a while longer, hoping they would just take what they came for and go, but that wouldn't happen anytime soon. The one-armed man turned his attention to the room we were in.

"I WANT EVERY ROOM IN THIS BUILDING CHECKED!" one robber shouts.

It's funny because I'm sure I heard that voice somewhere before. It sounded like Jason. He was due to get out three weeks after me. I looked over the filing cabinet to see if it was him, but all three were wearing masks. It was impossible to identify their faces.

Nonetheless, one of the robbers came closer to the door, and there was nowhere to hide, and I didn't bother trying either.

The robber got closer to us and then opened the door.

The robber had a quick reaction, pointing his gun at us, and then shouting,

"GET OUT HERE NOW."

I wasn't going to stand there arguing with him, he had the gun, and he was calling the shots. I walked towards him, both my arms in the air. The leader came walking towards me and craned his head,

"Anthony... is that you?" he asks, a note to surprise in his voice.

"Err, yeah... that's me?"

He removes his mask and looks right at me, and says,

"Boy, oh, boy, am I glad to see you!"

He came up to me with open arms, hardly surprised as we did get on rather well in jail.

"Is this where you shoot me in the back?" I ask.

"No, don't be silly... What the hell are you doing here anyway?" he asks.

"Well... I was going to open a loan account till you showed up, now I guess I am really without money now." I laughed.

He turned his attention to the young lady that was going to set up an account for me.

"Come forward, lady."

She steps forward, scared and shaken, and she looks as if she is about to wet herself. I felt sorry for her, but the problem is, she knows

I know them, and that would be a big problem for me. I can't afford to be exposed for the crimes I have committed.

"P-please, d-don't kill me,"

"I'm going to ask you a question, and I want you to be honest with me; once you tell me the truth, I will let you walk right out that front door with no harm to you. So, was your intention to open, Anthony, a loan account?"

"I- I was going to credit C-check him F-first,"

"Well, well, well, **ANTHONY!**"

At that point, I knew he was being sarcastic with her. He points the gun right at her head,

"P-please N-no, n-no, d-don't kill me."

He pulled the fucking trigger. The sound of the gun popped off in slow motion and echoed throughout the bank's lobby area. I looked to my right, and she dropped to the floor like a sack of shit. I was paralyzed on the spot while my eyes met her eyes. She was dead.

"See, she wasn't going to open you a stupid account, Anthony,"

"I would have killed her myself, to be honest. The last thing I need is the cops sniffing around me." I replied.

He opens a bag full of cash and says,

"You got a car?"

"Err, yeah, why?"

He throws me twenty thousand dollars and says,

"Get us the fuck out of here, and I'll give you ten thousand more."

My heart went numb, I wanted to leave the criminal life behind me, but at the same time, the money looked easy enough.

"Fine, let's move."

We all walked out of the bank like the five brothers. No police cars, no alarms sounding off. It looked easy. Yet, we went straight for my car, but, seconds away from getting in the car, one guard ran out of the bank shouting his mouth off,

"SOMEONE CALL THE COPS. THERE'S BEEN A ROBBERY!"

Jason then runs up to him, strikes him across the head with the butt of his gun, and drags him to my car. *Here we go again.*

Moments later, I was driving back to my place with the security guard in the boot of my car, but something concerned me even more—the security cameras in the bank.

"Jason, did you guys not think about the security system?"

"Yeah, we took the tape and destroyed the security system; we planned the whole thing. Don't worry; you will be fine, Anthony."

Yet, something didn't seem right... if they planned it, why would they need me to drive them away? Nonetheless, we made it out of the area and back to my place in one piece.

CHAPTER THIRTEEN

He cried so hard that he knelt, begging for his pathetic little life. He was so desperate, desperate to live. He wanted to live so badly to see his wife and child again, but I shot him where he knelt. I didn't have a care in the world. I just kept on shooting. I just kept on reloading. The only thing that kept me pulling that trigger was the thought of Laura in the back of my mind. I couldn't tell how many bullets entered his chest, but that last bullet? That entered through his right eye. It was dark red, pooling with blood, already blackening.

The remaining eye remained open, staring blankly at me. Some of his brains exploded from the back of his skull and splattered all over my perfectly white kitchen floor. The body had slumped to the floor like some ungainly life-sized doll. I stood there holding my gun, just staring back at him.

I didn't want to kill him. I didn't ask for this to happen. If I had let him go, I would lose everything, and I'm not going back to jail. Laura was due back, but after receiving a text message after our conversation, she said she needed to be by herself for a while.

I wasn't too sure what she meant by that. I checked her Facebook every few minutes just so I could engage with her in some banter, maybe?

Between times I did my research on topics she liked so that I could be more informed, more enjoyable, and more remarkable than her so-called friends. But then I can barely look at her posts after seeing her flirting with other guys. I could snap her pretty little neck in two. She's just a toy, really, but boys can be so protective about their toys, can't they? I never felt so pissed off in my life. The anger was building up more and more after seeing her comments on random guy's photos,

"YOU STUPID LITTLE BITCH!"

I placed the gun on the kitchen side because that thought made me feel things I didn't want to feel. I knew there was something in that shout, a pain behind it. I took another look at my gun, tempted to end my life where I stood. My hands were slowly reaching out to it. I felt my body had been overtaken by something.

"NO!"

I picked up the wine bottle on the kitchen side just by my gun. That's when I threw it against the wall. The loud bang left a hole in the wall, the thump of the flying wine bottle I threw, and the crash of the pieces coming into contact with the floor. Yet, I dropped to my knees and broke down on the kitchen floor. The anger was supposed to be a shield for my pain, but the pain had broken through it. I wish I could turn my tears off.

My emotions swirl like ocean currents, deep and robust. Yet, I'm here all alone. No one was here to pat me on the back and tell me everything will be OK. That's what made me angrier. I stood from kneeling on the floor as I glanced at the handgun for a moment longer before picking it back up. Would it just be easy to end it all now? The temptation wasn't finished with me; it felt like Karma had found its way into my life, ordering me to top it all. I placed my hands on each side of my hips, arching my back for a good stretch. I took one look at the corpse in front of me, wondering what I was going to do with it. Nonetheless, I began to wrap his body in Clingfilm. The only way I was getting rid of his body was at the bottom of the deep harbour waters. That's when I waited for time to pass.

Night had fallen. No more than an hour ago, the sky was red and orange, but all the colour faded, leaving only a black night. The darkness and myself all that seemed to exist was the chill and that harsh bite I could feel through my coat as I stepped out of my car. I stopped off at a restaurant to grab some coffee before ditching the body that was still in the boot of my car. The restaurant had a late breakfast deal. I hadn't eaten all day, so I may grab something to eat before heading to the Harbor.

I walked inside and saw dirty square tables, glass tops, menus with coffee stains, and slow-turning ceiling fans above. They were 80's classic jazz music playing in the background which was probably the only good thing going for this place. Yet, the waiters took my eye too; they were badly dressed in black and white uniforms that didn't look clean, or their uniforms never got cleaned or pressed. The terracotta rustic tiled floor looked like it hadn't been cleaned in a while, and the large windows that I could see had a small crack going down the middle.

God help that person when they lean on that. The small vases of yellow carnation flowers on each table looked badly presented. The only thing that did look right was the daily specials on a chalkboard at the entrance. It wasn't even busy at all.

I saw only five people sitting at the tables eating disgusting food. Yet, very unhealthy fat could be seen dripping off the overcooked burgers! I debated if I should even order a piss coffee, let alone a heart attack.

"Can I help you?" a waiter asks.

I looked around but was still put off by the amount of fat dripping from a burger that one oversized man was getting his teeth into.

"Sir, are you ordering with us?" he asks again.

"Sorry, do you really serve this crap?" I ask.

"PARDON?" a note to surprise in his voice.

"I'm sorry it's been a long day. I lean closer to the waiter. "but seriously, do you really serve this shit?"

"Well, what does it look like to you? Look, I hate my job, okay, but it puts great food on my table, obviously way better than this junk, so please buy something or fuck off."

I didn't blame him for his tone of voice; I would be just as pissed off or worse if anyone spoke to me the way I did to him.

"Well, just a piss coffee, please,"

"Piss coffee coming up."

The waiter stands there with a coffee jug and pours some into a cup. I wasn't wrong; It was piss coffee.

"Have you ever thought about becoming someone rather than settling for this dead-end job?" I ask.

"No, have you?"

"Not really, I just kill people,"

"Ha-ha, hilarious, wise guy."

He wasn't fazed by what I just said to him, and I don't know why I just said that. Maybe I was tired of hiding what I do, or perhaps it's a cry for help, or it's becoming part of me? I know one thing, though: I can feel a lot of pain inside, waiting for someone to come along and put me out of my misery.

"Seriously though; have you ever thought about it?"

"I hardly get time to stop and think about anything. My typical life is just routine, and I go home, shower, eat and sleep,"

"Fuck, you are a boring shit... no wonder you don't have a lady!"

"How would you know if I don't have a lady?"

I took one look at him and said,

"It's obvious."

I couldn't imagine living a life like his. I think I would've killed myself in the first week of stepping in his shoes. He took a seat and continued to speak while I sat there sipping on a cheap brand of piss coffee, listening to his bland life story as he sat there before me. I felt sorry for him despite his bland conversation. He was a decent guy, though, but a troubled soul like me. Yet, my eyes wandered over his left shoulder towards the clock on the far end of the wall. It was getting late.

"Listen, I have to get going, but think about what I said. You could be so much more than this place."

He sat there wondering in thought, like he was thinking, taking in what I had said. He looked right at me, eyes wide open like he'd been smacked with a fish. He then says,

"You know what... your right, man, fuck this place."

He stood from sitting and shouted,

"FUCK THIS PLACE, I'M GOING TO MAKE SOMETHING OF MYSELF."

He just dropped everything and took his feet to the exit, and he was gone, gone out of sight. I never expected that to happen. It wasn't my intention to make him quit right now, but he made a choice that many are afraid to make. I guess the guy needed a kick up the backside to make him realize what he was missing.

CHAPTER FOURTEEN

The roads were blackened by night, and hardly any cars could be seen. Occasionally you would see the odd vehicle pass by and a few drunk crawlers walking the streets shouting at themselves while fighting with bushes because they were so drunk that they hadn't a clue what they were doing or where they were. Nonetheless, I took a left into the harbour just a few miles from downtown. Yet, no one was around to witness me dumping the guy I shot. The headlights of my car reflected in the water. I stopped my car, switched off the engine, and looked out to the harbour waters. Every boat on the seas was beautifully lit up. They were so pretty that when the fleet set out into the night, I just sat there watching peacefully. I felt relaxed. But, I was here to do one thing, dispose of a body. I took one deep breath and then stepped out of my car and walked towards the deep waters. I looked around a few times.

No one was around but me. It felt like a graveyard. The stillness sent shivers down my spine. They were water dripping from the roof of the harbour warehouse, rhythmically generating a sad melody. Most of the warehouses looked abandoned. The door hinges were all rusted up, and the glass windows were shattered into millions of pieces, like my future dreams. I looked over the railings and down into the deep waters.

This was the best place to dump him. I casually walked back to my car when my eyes wandered off for a moment longer. I needed to make sure that no one was around before I popped open my car's boot. It seems no one is around. I opened the boot, grabbed his feet, and dragged him onto the floor. That's when paranoia set in.

I felt like a geek that was shot up on so much caffeine looking everywhere like an anxious nerd. I grabbed his legs again and pulled him across the wet concrete floor.

I was still paranoid. My eyes were still wandering off while I dragged him towards the railing. He was fucking heavy due to the heavy rocks I placed inside his clothing. The last thing I needed was a floating corpse with Anthony's name written all over him.

I looked over the railings and down into the waters for the last time before throwing him over. I hoped in my mind that he would sink. In the movies, drowning is loud and splashy, someone yells and waves their arms, and they dip below the waves and come up dramatically while those on shore scramble to rescue them. Ha-ha, this wasn't going to happen for him. I then threw him over and waved him off. I waited until he sunk below. I waited for an hour at least. By then, he was gone, and that's what I liked to see, no floating corpse and no trace. I looked around, making sure nothing was left behind. I casually walked back to my car when I received a text; it read,

"I left you a note back at your place."

That was it. No kisses. No nothing. This sounded off alarm bells in my head.

Yet, I was driving; softly splashing rain hit my car bonnet as I went onwards. I watched the raindrops race down the window. The occasional wave of a puddle can be exciting, but I'd rather be home in the warm than stuck in this car any longer. Where is my life leading? I ask myself this question time and time again. I was depressed. I was like a child again, scared of the outcome and how my life would end. I regret everything I did, for what? What have I achieved? What purpose do I have now? I thought about handing myself in, but I knew I would soon regret it the minute I walked through the door.

Yet, I reached deep inside the glove box and took out a pack of cigarettes. I took one out and charged up the car lighter. While I was patiently waiting for that to pop, I tried to find at least something decent on the radio, but nothing interested me.

The car lighter clicked, ready for me to light up my cigarette. Smoking was the only thing that calmed me down.

Thoughts crossed my mind and made me realize that I was on my own and had no one to turn to. The thoughts were so intense that I burned my cigarette in under a minute. I stubbed out my cigarette butt and began texting Laura while watching the road.

"*I can't wait to see you again, Laura. I miss you like crazy.*"

I kept overthinking while driving. I was fine for one minute, but there was a problem with me. Was it wrong to hate those who tried to understand me? What is the point of trying? I'm merely doing what I please. I couldn't love the idiots the world provided, but Laura is different. I have emotions like everyone else. They are just too stupid to see it.

Should I have a heart for those I have hurt to get where I am? I merely grasp opportunity when given and nothing less. Too many accept so little when they could have more. We are like little children biting our tongues to keep the truth sealed away. What a pathetic world we live in.

I was five minutes away from home; I drove up the hill back to my cabin. I took a steady right into my driveway when I noticed Laura's note flapping like crazy in the wind. I placed the handbrake on, turned off the engine, and stepped out of my car. I slowly walked towards my front door. I was standing just an inch away from the note as it freely tried to fly away. The only thing that stopped it from flying away was a pin holding it in one place. I took the note off and read it; *Anthony, I stopped by to talk with you in person, but you were out. I will be*

honest with you, you're a nice guy, but I really can't see you anymore. I'm sorry. Love from Laura.

"HOW THE HELL CAN SHE USE THE WORD LOVE?" I shout.

The paper crumpled as my fingers clenched into a fist, throwing away the paper ball. She is going to regret this. I unlocked the door and stepped inside. I stood by the door, looking around the cabin. It felt empty and cold. I knew somehow that Laura was going to walk out of my life. I could feel it when she flirted with the other guys on her Facebook. Well, I am disappointed in her. I had so much anger inside me right now, and I knew I needed to let off some steam. I shut the door behind me and went straight into the living room and rested my head on the couch until sunrise struck again. But as I slept through the night, I began to form a sweat.

I felt irritated. I had the worst night's sleep in history. I sat up, covering my face with my hands, and gently wiped the sweat dripping from my forehead.

I wouldn't say I like this feeling. The nightmares were getting worse. At times I felt I couldn't cope with them. The dreams consisted of me rather drowning or me falling from a great height, but my thoughts soon switched when I heard a loud thud on my front door. It didn't sound enjoyable either.

The thud made me reach under the couch, feeling around for my gun; that's when my fingertips touched the butt of the weapon. My door was then beaten down before I could get a good grip on the weapon.

"POLICE. SHOW YOURSELF!"

That's when I desperately grabbed the gun as fast as I could. I could hear heavy footsteps echoing towards me. That's when everything happens so quickly. I stood up and looked straight ahead. I saw several lights from the officer's torch dancing freely on the walls, ceilings, and floor. As I watched the lights from the torches dance freely, one cop rushed into the living room, where I stood, pointing my gun at his chest. I didn't have time to think about my actions. I pulled the trigger, and a hail of bullets peppered the room's walls, filling the air with thick clouds of dust, gunpowder, and an acrid, smoky odor. The cop didn't even get a chance to take a glimpse of me. I knew I was officially a cop killer when he hit the floor right then.

Every cop ran towards the downed officer, but I soon pulled the trigger on every cop that came through the door, only to take a bullet to my right leg and stomach. I noticed a dozen more bullets whizzed over my head, slamming into the wall and fireplace behind me. It took a minute before everything fell into silence. ***Well, that escalated quickly.***

I craned my head, listening out for any sound or movement from outside. The only thing I could hear was police sirens from a distance. That's when I knew it was time to leave. Every cop in the state was now hunting for me. I didn't bother packing an overnight bag because this place is now my past. I just picked up my car keys walked towards the front door.

Yet, I could see bright flashing lights coming from the abandoned police cruisers parked outside my cabin. They were seven police cruisers in total but not a single cop. I killed every cop. The sound of the sirens was getting closer at this point. I was staggering over to a police cruiser nearest to my left.

I looked through the car window looking around for supplies. ***I'll take that.*** I leaned inside the open window and took the 12-gauge shotgun and the first aid kit resting on the passenger seat of the cruiser. I needed all the weapons and first aid I could get my hands on. I didn't know what I would do or where I was going next, but I needed shelter to lick my wounds. I staggered over to my car, opened the back passenger door, and threw in the 12-gauge shotguns on the back seat. I shut the door, got into the driver's seat, and reversed onto the road. I investigated my rear-view mirror and saw the flashing lights fast approaching at speed. That's when I sped off before they caught sight of me. I was driving, thinking about where I was going to stay. My life was a complete mess.

After driving around while being cautious, I found a place I could stay, but only for a short while. From outside, the boarded windows and the shabby wood panelling and the door sealed with iron rods all looked threatening enough to keep people away.

The building looked ancient and rusty, fit to fall apart with a single touch. One deep breath to ease my pain, and I slowly put my foot on the step. I froze in discomfort. I couldn't work out whether this place was an old office building? Well, that's what it looked like from the outside. Nonetheless, I forced the door open and stepped inside. Nothing but the darkness around me was present. I couldn't stop thinking about Laura. I needed her so bad, but hell could I do now? I was on the run. She wouldn't want me now. Maybe I could kidnap her? I stood there constantly thinking about my next move, but I realized I was bleeding out. I had forgotten I had a bullet stuck in my leg and stomach. I walked over to the wall, pressed my back against it, took off my coat, and threw it onto the floor. After that, I slowly lifted my blood-stained shirt.

The bullet wound was causing such a nasty pain. The pain throbs in my guts and my leg. It's deep and warm, and not pleasant. It feels like someone has their hand squeezing my organs and crushing my leg. I can only keep still and breathe, breathe slowly and deeply until it passes. I was scared. I didn't waste any more time. I had the first aid with me. I sat on the floor with my back resting against the wall. I opened the first aid box. My hands were shaking so severely that all the first aid came flying out of the box and all over the floor in the dark. ***I don't need this bullshit right now.***

Nonetheless, I picked it up and began to clean and dress both my wounds. I was so tired that after I patched myself up, I felt myself falling asleep while watching my own pale hands dance. I was out for the count.

CHAPTER FIFTEEN

It was early morning, 7:00. The sun penetrated through the tiny rectangle window above the front door. I slept there, ensuring no person was coming through that door. If they tried, they would have my 12-gauge shotgun pointing in their face. The pain from the womb seemed to have calmed down a little, it throbs time to time, but it was easing off. I wasn't sure about my next move. I was scared to step outside that door, knowing I had the whole state looking for me. I reached into my jacket and took out my cell phone. ***Great, no signal.*** I stood from sitting on the floor and walked about to see if I could somehow get a signal so I could track down Laura. I thought long and hard about what I was going to do... I was planning to kidnap her. But where would we go? I needed somewhere out of the city, but I had no money because I forgot to pick it up. All I had was my cell phone, car, first aid for when I needed it, and two shotguns... not to forget my smokes. Yet, I felt hopeless, nowhere for Laura and me to live.

Every time I closed my eyes, that's when I saw her face. When I see her, it's as if space became the most delicate point imaginable; it's as if my universe begins and ends with her. I could run from the cops forever, search for her forever, but sometimes, every path leads to the end of the road... but I will not have that thought go through my mind just yet. I was tempted to head on out, but I had no one, and I was too weak. I knew I had to wait this out until I could walk.

I needed to remain in the shadows until the heat died down. I had white knuckles from clenching my fist too hard, and I couldn't stop grinding my teeth from the lack of effort to remain silent. My face was red with suppressed rage. I swung around and mentally snapped, kicking and punching the walls. I couldn't get a darn signal on my cell phone. I felt stupid losing it the way I did over a cell phone. Nonetheless, I didn't particularly want to wait out in a building full of dust and smashed-out windows; it drove me insane. I had been pacing back and forth like a caged tiger for the last twenty minutes going through thoughts in my head. There it went again, and my anxiety started to talk even louder. The anxiety's not my friend at all. It speaks to me; ***Everything has gone wrong, no way back now, disaster strikes, run away.*** The world was closer to my eyes, and the air was heavier and harder to breathe at times. A fuzzy feeling coats my eyes; It wasn't there before? Yet, my thoughts scatter like a storm raging in my head; too many short circuits to make any sense. All the while, the thoughts in my head said a few things; ***You're failing, it's over, give up, run away.***

Maybe my anxiety was right. Perhaps I should just give up? I walked towards the exit of the abandoned building and opened the door when my eyes were squinting against the sunlight that was beaming down onto my face. I looked around outside, and the world was still sleeping. I knew I couldn't just walk around freely as I could. I knew I had to wait this out even though I was tempted to leave this place. I went back inside, sat down just by the door, and decided to wait it out.

Time passed as I sat patiently. It was ten at night; I looked above me as the light came on randomly? I don't just see the bulb flicker; I hear it too. I'm not sure if it's the bulb or the bad electrics. All I know is... I don't want to be in here when the light goes out. This building is creepy enough in the daylight, with cracked walls and bleeding moisture from the earth outside. I was depressed. I could use a stiff drink right now. That's when I decided to head out to a bar or club. Either way, I wasn't bothered which bar they both sell alcohol in.

That's when I stood from sitting on the floor by the door. I opened the door and walked straight to my car. The funny thing is I didn't hide my car last night. Stupid old fool that I am at times. I got to the driver's side, switched on the engine, and sped off. I couldn't explain the feeling I was getting while driving around, knowing that I could be caught by the cops any minute.

I wasn't clever at all. I was careless, but my father always used to say that being careless is sometimes intelligent; I never really understood what he meant by that? I still struggle to understand that to this day.

Nonetheless, I took a left into a parking lot in the downtown area. It was late, and people were hyped up outside a club. I parked up and switched off the engine to my car. I sat longer for a moment, just gazing across the street at the crowd queuing up to get inside the club.

I couldn't help but notice how the men would just look at the women like they were sex objects. I could read their minds, and that bothered me. Yet, I stepped out of my car and walked across the street. I could feel the crowd's eyes burning me as I got closer to them. I wasn't paranoid, although they were a slight possibility. But it was amazing. It was the first time that I had been to a club. Inside the club, they were blue, acid greens, hot pinks, and gold lights beaming all over the place. The music played over the dance floor fused with everyone. I sat at the bar with no money. I wasn't sure how I was going to get a drink. I took out my smoke and lit one up. I slowly turned my head to my left when I saw a woman standing there with her right hand on her hip. She then called me,

"Excuse me, sir,"

I felt like I was being forced to look into her eyes; that's when I could see her emotions were not easily hidden on her innocent face.

Her eyes were, without doubt, the fascinating aspect of her appearance, and yet she showed her soul, bad or good... I couldn't tell just yet. I was still looking into her eyes when I saw Laura staring back at me. Laura... the brightest fire in my life, and one that won't burn out so quickly. I shook my head to vanish Laura from my mind. Yet this woman was so inviting, that's when I knew I had to speak to her,

"Can I help you?" I reply.

"I'm so sorry to ask this, but... do you have a smoke I could have, please?"

I needed a drink, and she needed a smoke... we need to trade.

"Well, if you can help with a stiff drink, I can help you with two clouds of smokes; how's that sound?"

She looked as if she was in profound thought.

"Err... I suppose that sounds fair, but only one drink."

She had a great body, great arse too. She was about 5-4 in height, and her weight looked maintained too. Her hair was light blond, down to her breasts.

"Of course, just one," I wink.

"You have a name?" she asks.

"Anthony is my name; what about you?"

"Laura." She offers to shake my hand at that point.

YOU HAVE TO BE KIDDING ME! I froze, speechless, to say the least. Is everyone called Laura nowadays? I just can't seem to shake her from my life. That's when I gently kissed the back of her hand like a gentleman. She smiled and got me a drink.

"Here you go, handsome,"

She slightly slides the glass of whiskey to her left and says,

"If you down that, I'll buy you another and maybe fuck you back at my place."

I couldn't help but wonder if she would be alone or with some friends. That's when I gazed around before necking back the shot of whiskey and slamming the empty glass down as a finisher move.

"**WOW**. I guess I owe you another drink and a fuck, mister."

Her giggle built up inside her; it sounded like a braying donkey.

"How is this funny?" I ask.

"I'm sorry, but you don't look like a drinker?"

"Oh, I really am, trust me..."

"Okay, I believe you... Ready for round two?"

"Sure, why not."

We continued to drink throughout the night and talk about life.

I got to know a lot about her too. She was single, with no children, and an accountant manager for some bank in the downtown area.

Nonetheless, time passed. At the night's end, the dance floor was like an abused street with rubbish everywhere, spilt drinks, and broken glass all over the floor with the lights up for the cleanup scene.

I couldn't help but admire such a mess; Like how can human beings just live like shit and not have a care in the world? Nonetheless, Laura leaned closer to me, just inches away from my face, as she looked deep into my eyes with such a seductive look on her face... she said,

"Say, I'm a little scared to walk back to my apartment on my own She bits her bottom lip. "Do you mind helping a girl out?"

I felt overpowered by her as she had already made up her mind.

"Sure, why not,"

"I just live a few blocks away; we can walk from here and cut through the central park?"

"You always cut through the park at this time of night?"

"Yes... wait... are you scared?" a note to surprise in her voice.

"Of course not. It's just I have a car, so why walk?"

"Because you are drunk, stupid."

We walked towards the exit when she linked her arm to mine. We were like a drunken couple just chuckling like we hadn't been let out in a while.

We exited the club when a loud voice shouted from across the street,

"HEY, YOU!" a guy calls from across the street.

"Not that guy again," she nervously spoke.

"This guy bothering you?"

"Yeah, he is my landlord, I kind of owe him money, and he just doesn't seem to get the hint that I don't have the money right now,"

"Do you want me to have a word with him?"

"I can't expect you to do that."

I walked across the street while Laura stood there with a nervous look. If I can calm the situation without killing the guy, then that's better for me. But the look on his face said otherwise.

"YOU BEST TELL THAT BITCH TO HAND OVER MY MONEY RIGHT NOW, OR I WILL CRACK HER JAW!"

His shout was violence in the air. He didn't just raise his voice, his fist clenched as if he was ready to land a left, his arms tensed, and he got right in close for maximum impact. I didn't even get to say a word; I was way too drunk for this. I really couldn't be bothered to stand there and wait for whoever made the first move. To be honest, I felt powerful. I felt I could end him where he stood. I mean that would be the end of her problems, and no one was around to see it. The only thing I saw was a threat. He wanted to get to her, but I didn't allow that.

I reached into my jacket and pulled out a knife. The knife I was holding was a single piece of high carbon stainless steel, hand-honed and about four inches long. I'm already wanted by the cops, so this didn't matter to me. I guess I wanted to do her a favour. As I was twisting the blade in my right hand, I thought about how killing become easier for me, like I felt some kind of thrill doing it. Of course, I was in denial. Wouldn't you be? I could already see him in a pool of darkening blood with his face split into a grin.

But then I felt the knife slowly slip from the palm of my hand and into hers. Laura ran up to him. The knife met his flesh and made a satisfying impact as the blade's tip sank deep enough to make him scream like a girl. She twisted the blade in her hands, sinking it deeper and deeper. The skin on her hand was torn to shreds as the knife rotated,

"YOU WILL NEVER ASK ME FOR RENT AGAIN!"

Then without warning, she jerked it into his upper left chest until the shiny metal had disappeared inside him.

I smirked like I was proud of her. Like I was teaching a cub how to catch its first meal, but as he fell to the floor, Laura sank to her knees and screamed, convulsing and trembling like a rabid animal. I walked over to her and pulled her off the floor, and I persistently said,

"We need to get out of here."

I held on to her arm as we quickly returned to my car. I opened the front passenger door and said,

"Get in and stay there."

She didn't hesitate. I walked back over to the dead guy. I grabbed each arm and dragged his corpse across the street to my car. I pulled his body past the passenger's side of my car when I saw Laura gazing at his body. She knew she had killed someone, but she didn't know how to accept it. Yet, I opened the boot and threw him in like he was nothing but meat. After that, I closed the boot, zipped up my jacket, stretched my body, and blew into my hands to keep warm. I looked up into the sky, studying it for a moment longer; I knew the rain was no more than a few minutes away.

CHAPTER SIXTEEN

T he motel was one of those nasty places where men went to fuck other wives. ***Isn't that a swingers club I'm thinking of?*** Outside the motel, weeds grew through the concrete floor, and the litter boxes from decade take-out meals were scattered across it. This place had no pride. Yet, external metal stairs led to the second floor of the motel rooms. It's the best I'm going to get for now.

We couldn't go back to Laura's place because she hadn't spoken a single word to me all night. It's like her soul just left her body. I wasn't this bad when I made my first kill. I guess I will have to comfort her until she learns. Nonetheless, I sat on the edge of the bed a few feet away from the window.

I heard a car door slam. Is this trouble that I didn't need right now? I stood from sitting on the bed and walked over to the window, cautiously peeking through the small gap in the curtain while squinting against the morning sun. That's when I saw two cops sniffing around my car. This was big trouble. This was bad.

"SHIT!"

That's when Laura shot out of bed faster than she could even put her knickers back on.

"What's wrong?" a note to surprise in her voice.

"We got cops sniffing around my car,"

"They know we're here, don't they?" she panics.

I looked deep into her eyes. That's when I witnessed the fright inside her soul. She hadn't a clue that I was a killer, nor did she know I was wanted for a string of murders longer than my arm. Yet, she will learn about me. They were something about her that struck my mind, and that wasn't because her name was Laura. That first kill she did, I could see whom she was becoming by looking deep into her eyes. We aren't that different... only that I have more experience than her.

"You may have to kill again," I say.

"Please don't let them take me," she says tremblingly.

"You may need to kill again,"

"Oh God, no." her voice was drowning in tears.

"Not again,"

"Shit happens, lady."

I wasn't going to just wrap her up in cotton wall. She needed to understand what it's like to be a killer. She killed someone, and she needs to embrace that. Still looking out the window, I saw a woman walk over to one officer while the other officer was still sniffing around my car. I remember when I first saw that woman when I pulled into the motel last night. She looked at me like she had seen my face before. I suppose my mug shot was all over the News.

"You're the one with the guns," she remarks.

I began to scan the area for more cops. It seemed they were only two cops. I could see the woman still talking to one officer, but she pointed to our room. The officer gazed up at me once and slowly clips his sidearm and shouted to his partner.

"CALL FOR BACKUP!"

That's when one officer made his way towards us and up the stairs. I looked at Laura and said,

"I guess your right... I am the one with the guns."

I massage my temples with the tips of my fingers, trying to rub away the headache that had just begun. I turned around and saw the shotgun in Laura's hand.

"Please deal with this calmly," she sarcastically says.

"Pleasure is all mine."

I took the shotgun from her and cocked it back once with one hand. I just wanted this over and done with.

"ANTHONY STONE, I KNOW YOU'RE IN THERE!" an officer shouts from the other side of the door.

"PISS OFF!" I replied.

Laura crouched at the side of the bed while my back was pressed against the door waiting for the officer to make his first and last move. The minute he comes through that door... he's a dead cop.

"ANTHONY, COME OUT WITH YOUR HANDS UP. DON'T MAKE THIS HARD FOR YOURSELF!"

I gave the cop his due, he was trying to find a peaceful resolution to this before it spirals out of control, which will happen eventually.

"PISS OFF COP!"

The stupid cop just kept on yapping and banging on the door. His voice went through me.

"Pass me the remote, will you," I say to Laura.

She picks up the remote that could be seen resting on the bottom of the bed and slowly walks over to me.

"You have a plan, right?" she hands me the remote.

"Nope, I just go with it."

I switched on the television and turned it up as high as it could go to drain the cop's voice. It felt great. I couldn't hear what they were saying.

"YOU MIGHT WANT TO FIND A LITTLE MORE COVER THAN A BED, SWEETHEART!" I winked. I didn't have a plan; I didn't know how to get out of this. I didn't want to stick around and wait for more cops to show up.

Two cops? This should be easy! That's when the party started. The cop then shouts from behind the door,

"I'M GOING TO GIVE YOU TO THE COUNT OF THREE, ONE. TWO..."

"FUCK IT, THREE!" I replied.

I opened the door and raised the shotgun, pointing at the officer's head that stood before me. His eyes were wide open as he stared down the barrel. Seconds felt like minutes. The only words that came out of his mouth were,

"FUCK!"

I pulled the trigger and took half his forehead clean off. Blood gushed from his head like a fountain before he dropped to the floor like a sack of shit. The gunbattle had started.

The motel complex went from quiet to a crowded stadium within a second, and people were running from their rooms. That's when I opened fire on every single fucker I saw.

"I MAY AS WELL MAKE A BIG DEAL OUT OF THIS!" I shout.

I looked back into our room when I saw her crouching.

"No time for that, sweetheart!" I sarcastically say.

She stood from cowering and walked slowly behind me as we proceeded out of our room. That's when the other officer caught eyes on me and opened fire.

"PUT THE WEAPON DOWN, ANTHONY!"

"I CANT. IT'S GLUED TO MY FUCKING HAND, AND YOU KEEP SHOOTING AT ME!"

I fired a few shots over the railings, peppering the floor from the impact of the bullets just missing the officer. That's when the officer took cover behind my car. I looked at Laura and said,

"Stay here while I kill this fucker."

I made my way towards the stairs while still firing at anyone I caught my eyes on. Why? I just felt the urge to make a big deal out of this and take as many lives as possible before this fucker takes me down. I would rather be remembered for who I am, not for what I did.

"Here, piggy, piggy," I call.

I walked over to my car and fired a few rounds, inches away from where the officer was hiding.

"Come on now. Show yourself, piggy."

The cop stood from hiding behind my car and said,

"P-please. W-wait."

The officer was scared, and his voice expressed that. He held his gun in the air and slowly emerged away from my car. He looked at me and threw his gun on the ground and kicked it towards me with his left foot without my instructions. I knew what he was planning. Keep me talking while the backup arrives? Fuck that. I raised my shotgun, aiming it at his chest. But I craned my head to the side as I watched him piss himself.

"How the fuck did you become an officer of the law? Let me help you with the waterworks down there, my friend."

I pulled the trigger. He didn't even blink. I'm starting to love shotguns. It left a hallmark in the officer that was on the floor. He was still alive, surprisingly. I casually walk over to him, peering over him. His eyes met mine as he cried in agony.

"P-please. I didn't see you. G- Go."

"Sweet dreams."

I shot him for the last time. After I put the poor bastard out of his misery, I looked around for a moment longer.

The motel complex was full of bodies; some bodies could be seen on the stairs, and some bodies hanging over the railings and all over the floor. I sure caused a lot of mess, but the silence was welcomed afterwards. Laura leans over the railing nearest to the stairs and says,

"What the fuck have you done." a note to surprise in her voice.

"What?" I look around. "They pissed me off." I shrug my shoulders.

Laura walks slowly down the stairs with a devilish smirk on her face. I couldn't help but admire her as she bit her bottom lip like this was the Laura I wanted, evil as me and twisted as fuck. I was confused with love.

"So, you kill everyone?"

"Well, that wasn't the plan, but I guess the answer to your question would be...**FUCK YEAH!**"

She stands next to me, looking around at the mess I did, and says,

"Well, your car is definitely done for."

The tire to my car was fucked, and there was no way that was going anywhere.

"Oh my, that is a beauty!"

I happily scream like a child eating candy.

I saw a saloon nicely parked in front of the main office. Everything shot up but not a scratch on that beauty.

"Isn't it nice being on the run? You can practically take whatever you want, my dear." I sarcastically say.

She rolled her eyes and said,

"Let's just get out of here."

CHAPTER SEVENTEEN

No home, no cash, but I have a beautiful car out of it... for as long as I need, not to mention Laura. Laura, soon to be a killer just as greater as me, almost. We drove for hours along the desert roads almost out of gas. The bitch wouldn't quit moaning about how I messed up her life. How naive is she? She is a great person but immature. At times she acted like a hooker. She wouldn't stop flirting with me. After moaning at me, she moved in closer to me as my eyes were on the road. She arched her back, reaching her lips to my ear, and whispered,

"Let's fuck."

Don't get me wrong, I like the idea, but I was more afraid of the cops catching me off guard. She continues to bite my ear gently. I liked it, but I wasn't in the mood.

"JUST STOP!"

She ignored it; she was persistent. She moved down to my stomach, continued further down, and began to unzip. She looks up at me and says,

"No, I promise you will like it." she winked.

That's when she slowly does it, just like she said she would. I hadn't felt that touch in a long time, and right now, I wasn't planning on pushing her off, at least until I was done. It felt good that I placed my hand flat on her head and pushed her head further down, harder until I reached my peak. I pulled over the car and said,

"Enough bull shit, come here."

She arched her back underneath the steering wheel as she slowly made her way up to my level. Her hair brushed up against my face. That's when she grabbed my throbbing cock and began to ride it. She loved it; I could tell. I loved every moment of her. I was getting right into it. I looked in the rear-view mirror when I saw a police cruiser pulled up behind us. That's when I pushed her off in a panic. I didn't even get to finish off.

"SHIT," I shouted.

"What's wrong?"

"We have a problem."

I investigated the rearview mirror for the last time. He was alone. The officer turns on his lights and lets off a single siren sound.

He then opens his car door, placing one leg out, followed by the other.

"He is a big fucker," I remark.

Laura laughed, but the laugh was a sign of her nerves. You could tell by her shaking hands dancing around as she reached for the cigarettes on the dashboard.

"Just play it cool and let me do the talking," I say.

"Why not just kill him?" she asked.

The officer casually walks up to the rear of my car, checking it over. That's when he reached for his flashlight and knocked out one taillight. He then looks behind. He slowly walks up to my window and gently taps on it with his flashlight. I thought about taking him down right then. I lowered my window and said,

"Can I help you, officer?"

He spits on the ground and says,

"You have a broken taillight and that my boy is a ticket."

He was smug. He was around six feet in height and close to being... overweight.

I leaned out the window, looking to the rear, and said,

"Geez, you don't say. I swear I just saw you do that?"

He stares hard, hoping for me to break and beg. Nope, not me. He grabbed me, dragged me out the car window, and threw me to the ground, repeatedly kicking me in the gut.

"THAT IS NO WAY TO SPEAK TO THE LAW, BOY. DIDN'T YOUR FATHER TEACH YOU ANY MANNERS, YOU PILE OF SHIT!"

As he continued to kick me in the gut, all I could hear was the sound of a shotgun. That's when I noticed the kicking had stopped. The constant kicking dazed me. I looked up, squinting against the sunlight that was blinding my view, and there she was, holding the shotgun with nerves like steel. She was hot.

"Well, you are a badass after all," I say.

I sat up from lying on the floor. That's when a few things began to enter my mind. We had hardly any gas and no place to stay.

"What do we do now?" she asks.

The thoughts crossed my mind a few times.

"Well, I sure could do with something to eat right now,"

"I know a great place, not far from here, but I'm driving."

I was in no fit state to be driving. I felt like a whole rugby team had charged at me. I stood from sitting on the ground and walked back to the car with Laura. That's when I noticed blood leaking from my stomach. Laura walked ahead and opened the car door, but she saw the blood on my shirt.

"Why are you bleeding?" a note to surprise in her voice.

That's when I collapsed to the floor, and before you know it, I was out cold.

CHAPTER EIGHTEEN

The hospital corridor was stuffy. The walls were scraped in places from the trolleys that had bumped into them. The pictures on the wall at the side of me looked like a cheap print. Above the double doors are large green signs with the areas of the hospital that lie ahead. I was lying there alone, freaking out. I had no clue where Laura was, but I was lying on a hospital bed with a drip attached to my arm. The hospital was busy, and I was just tossed to one side in a hospital corridor with nothing to do but look around at the dull walls. Yet, on a plastic hallway chair sat a child, legs kicking in the air, clearing the floor by several inches as they swung back and forth, he looked bored as hell, and I understood his frustration. That's when I saw a doctor walking up the corridor. *I sure hope this doc is here to see me.* The doctor walked towards the boy and said,

"Hey there, I'm Doctor James. What's your name?" The boy sat still and was quiet for a moment but sat further back into the chair.

I was curious about where Laura was, so I thought maybe this doctor would know, but I felt rude to intrude right now. That's when I saw her walking towards me holding two cups.

"Hey Alex, you OK?" Laura remarked.

"ALEX... WHO THE FUCK IS ALEX?"

The doctor that was speaking with the young boy looks back, confused.

"Alex, I will be right over in a moment."

I look at Laura, confused.

"Who am I?"

She laughs and whispers,

"Just go along with it, stupid."

For a moment, I started to believe I was Alex. I thought I had lost my mind.

"So, all the while we have some alone time, how about you tell me how you got the bullet wounds?" Laura asks.

"Now? Do you want me to tell you everything right now?

"Yeah, I suppose so." She shrugged her shoulders.

Where should I start is what I was thinking. I whisper to her in the hope no one will hear.

"Maybe when the walls don't have ears, then I can tell you, but the doc over there would call the cops in seconds if he heard anything,"

"The doctor did say an officer would need to be called in a situation like this?"

"Are you stupid?"

She looks right at me, surprised by my response, but soon realizes why. Two officers casually walk up the corridor. That's when she froze on the spot holding her cup. Her hand was shaking, and her cup was dancing, spilling onto the clean floor.

"Oh shit," she remarked.

"Time to leave. Help me with this, will you." I asked.

She placed her cup on the ground and took the drip out of my arm. I needed to think fast before the cops caught sight of me. But I was too late. One cop stared hard, right at me. That's when he whispers to his partner. The other cop then looks straight at me and pulls out his gun. It all happened so fast. I rolled off the bed onto the floor. That's when the cop opened fire. I grabbed Laura in panic.

All I heard was the snap of the bullets coming towards us. That's when Laura slips away from me. That moment she dropped to the floor, I grabbed the doctor and shouted,

"I'M WARNING YOU. IF YOU COME ANY CLOSER, I WILL SNAP HIS FUCKING NECK!".

I looked at Laura on the floor. She was dying, her eyes gazing in and out of consciousness as she looked at me, but she then said,

"R-run,"

"SHE NEEDS HELP. SOMEONE FUCKING HELP HER!"

That's when she smiled at me. She then died right in front of me. I couldn't think. I was confused. I knew the second I let this doctor go, I would be lying right next to her.

"SLIDE YOUR WEAPONS OVER TO ME, OR THE DOCTOR WILL DIE!"

"Okay, just calm down." An officer replied.

The cops slowly placed their weapons on the ground and slid them over. I looked at the young boy that was still sitting on the chair. He was scared.

"Hey, kid."

He looks up at me.

"Be a good kid and pick up the guns. I'm not going to hurt you."

He leaps off the chair and walks over to the guns a few feet away from me. The boy leans down and picks them both up. He then walks over to me and hands them to me. I made a split decision and took one of the guns. I knew there was only one way out of this. That's when I looked at the cops and said,

"I'm sorry about this."

I pointed the gun at the officers and pulled the trigger. They both then dropped to the floor. I went into thought. Everything around me somehow slowed down. My eyes were glued to the officers as I watched them slowly fall. It was a strange feeling. Can you imagine what I am seeing right now? Still watching them fall as their eyes were deep in thought, seconds away from their death. What were they thinking? What did they feel as they fell to the ground? I gazed around, watching everyone running and screaming in mass panic. That's when I made a split decision. I needed a way out.

I was walking through the hospital corridors trying to find a way out, and that's when I saw a man walking towards me playing with his car keys. I needed a ride. He walks past me. I turned around and stuck the gun in his back and said,

"You say anything, and I will pull the trigger and end your life. Got it?"

"I...I got it, sir,"

"Guide me to the exit and then to your car without making a scene, got it?"

"Yes, sir... it's right this way." He points onward.

He acts as expected and walks at my side towards the exit without making a scene as planned.

CHAPTER NINETEEN

The poor guy didn't stand a chance. I snapped his neck after he handed me the keys to his car. I was driving around thinking about how fucked up my life was. I wasn't sure what I was going to do, but I knew one thing, I needed to get the hell out of the United States, but that wasn't going to happen anytime soon.

Nonetheless, I was driving through the city thinking about Laura Edwards. In a way, I am happy to be on my own again. It meant I could concentrate on finding Laura again, and I didn't have to worry about babysitting someone that hadn't a clue about killing and escaping the law. She paid the price. She just wasn't clever enough.

I was sitting at the traffic lights waiting for them to turn green when I heard gunshots coming from the west bank. I watched armed men calmly walking out of the bank with a hostage. That's when I thought about Jason. I waited until they got inside a black pickup truck. I don't know what I was thinking, but I needed the money, and somehow, these guys knew exactly what they were doing. I had nothing left for me. No money, no home, no job, no nothing. I needed a way out. I waited until the black pick-up pulled out before tailing them. I sat there patiently waiting for the darn lights to change. That's when I made a split decision to go through the red light before I lost sight of them. I was never- great at tailing people. I continued to follow them when I found myself pulling up outside a junkyard.

I switched off the engine and sat there as the black pick-up truck slowly made its way into the junkyard that was heavily guarded by what looked to be professionally armed men. I was a little terrified after sighting the guards that stood by the junkyard entrance. People like this would kill you if they thought you were a threat.

I gazed around before getting out of my car as two guards shut the gate, ensuring no one watched them. It would be nice to knock on the Savaged junkyard gate and ask for a job. That reminds me, I remember when I was a kid, oh yeah, they were the days. The junkyard was where I used to go as a kid. I used to climb into the piled-high rusty cars like they were bunk beds and pretended I was driving while the rain railed against the cracked windshields and metalwork. They were the days I truly missed.

Nonetheless, I waited in my car as the clouds above began to open and night had begun. I'm not sure what my crazy head was up to. I guess I just went along with it.

I opened the door and stepped out. That's when I caught my eye on the junkyard gate opening again. I took cover on the other side of my car and watched as the black pick-up made its way to the exit. I couldn't get a good look at the men inside the black pickup- truck. The rain was belting it down, blinding my view. I lean up some more and begin squinting my right eye into focus. I still couldn't work out who was in the black pickup truck. That's when I suddenly felt the cold metal muzzle of a gun pressed against the back of my head. Next thing you know, I was out cold again.

I woke, squinting against the industry light standing in front of me. I knew I was in serious shit when I noticed my arms were stretched above my head, chained by my wrist to the raw concrete ceiling. I was naked and shivering. They stripped me, leaving only my pants to cover my dick. ***Thank God.*** I could just make out what the door in front of me was made from. It was a rusted steel door with two jail locks from the inside. Once locked inside, there was no way of getting out unless the nice chaps let me out or I somehow killed them both. I gazed around the room when I saw a man dead on the floor as blood was gushing from his neck and down into the drain. The room I was in was like some kind of meat room, sound- and escape-proof, and the walls and floor were tiled and a dirty white colour.

Nonetheless, I struggled a little to set myself free, but they did a great job chaining me up. I was awake for almost an hour, and I couldn't help but gaze at the dead guy.

"COME ON NOW, WILL YA," I shouted.

I was getting frustrated by the second. All I wanted was to explain myself better, maybe convince them to set me free and give me a job, or they could just beat me to death. I looked around for a moment longer. I heard two bolts unlocking from the other side of the door and one man opening from this side. Two heavily built men casually walk in, laughing among each other like I wasn't even there. I gasp when one of the men walks over to a chain wrapped around a large hook that was screwed deep into the wall, he slightly pulls the chain, causing me to rise a little more until my toes no longer touch the ground. The other guy was dragging the corpse across the room to a meat grinder. I guess that's where I will end up if I can't convince them I'm a killer like them.

"HEY, BIG GUY!" I shouted over to the guy wrapping the chain around the hook. That's when the other guy comes rushing over and says,

"Shhh." The man brought a finger to my lips and whispers

"You will die very slowly." His voice was cold.

"Oh yeah, how do you plan to do this? I can recommend some great ideas." I replied with no fear, although fear is what I was projecting deep inside, and he could tell. His hard stare was what gave me away.

"I'm starting to like this funny man already," he says to his pal standing by a switch nearest to the meat grinder. He flipped the switch, and the meat grinder gave off a loud buzzing noise like it was trying to grind up metal.

I saw a quick mist of blood gushing from the top.

My heart was hammering as I saw the dead corps coming out the other end of the grinder like mince you buy from a shop. I gasp once more before I say,

"Listen, I am no threat to you."

The other guy left the room, leaving his pal and me to work things out. What bothered me the most was when he walked over to me with this small trolley on wheels. It had a few tools on there that made me swallow hard. That's when I knew what it was like to be on the other end of being tortured.

"Who are you?" he asks.

"I'm a killer."

The man laughed a bizarre, gurgling laugh. That's when I saw him holding a nail gun in his left hand. He walked around the small table, and then he was inches away from my face and licked his cracked lips and smiled. That's when he whispers,

"Guess what," he quickly fires four nails into my left leg. I gasped in agony, and that's when I started to feel nausea flooding my gut. My vision blurred.

"You think I care how you feel right now? he says.

"I'm telling you the truth. I am like you. I kill people." I cry.

He walks back around, facing the trolley. He looks at the tools on the table, thinking about what he could use next.

"How many have you killed?" he asks.

"The truth is, I lost count. But I'm sure the FBI has my mug shot on their website, so why don't you see yourself?"

He placed the tools back on the trolley and said,

"What's your name?" he asked.

"Anthony Stone," I replied.

He turns around and wheels the table to the door and says,

"I will be back shortly; I hope that the FBI wants you for your sake. Oh, one last thing, what the hell are you even doing here?" his voice echoes. I couldn't even speak; I felt I was blacking out from the amount of pain shooting up my leg.

Hours passed, and I wasn't sure of the time, and the longer I was dangling, the more I thought my life was about to end. I heard the door unlock, and a man walked over to me. His face was covered so I couldn't see, but then he shouted,

"HOLY SHIT!"

Sure, I heard that voice before, but I was dazed. He walked over to the chain wrapped around the hook and released it, causing me to drop to the floor. He rushed over to me and leaned down, removing the mask that covered his face. At that moment, I was happy to see Jason's face,

"You are one lucky son of a bitch," he remarked.

Right then, I knew what he said was true. I'd hate to think what would've happened to me if he didn't know anything. That's when he looks deep into my eyes and says,

"Welcome to the family; now you have to prove you're worthy to the boss, but if you don't, then it's not down to me if you live or die."

He wasn't harsh to me. I could see the pain when he said that. That's when I knew I was in deep over my head.

"All I wanted was to make some money and see Laura again,"

"Listen, man, you need to forget about this girl. She is nothing but trouble, and you'll see this in the end."

The things he said made me think long and hard about Laura. He almost convinced me she was a waste of time. The only thing that was on my mind was that I am pretty much a nobody. I have no home, money, job, and no girl on my arm. I needed to change, and maybe it's for the best to let Laura go and live her life, even if that means being with someone else. Ah, who am I trying to kid here? All the shit I have gone through to be with her? I can't just give up on her, not now.

"I mean what I say, she is trouble man. I mean, look at yourself. You are a mess,"

"What?"

"What do you mean what? Can't you see what she has done to you, even though she has no clue she is doing it? Look, Anthony, you are the one with the fucked-up head. Sort yourself out."

My past, my action, and everything that I did just to be with her made me realize just how crazy I am over her. He was right. Even if I tried, it would be impossible.

CHAPTER TWENTY
THREE YEARS LATER

The man has the swagger of someone I don't even want to lock eyes with, let alone mess with. His arms are more ink than skin, and his black hair was so closely cropped that I had mistaken him for being bald from a distance. I decided to busy myself tidying the garage tools, but that's when he hails me outside, the kind of tone you don't ignore if you like breathing without a respirator. After so many years of running this joint, you know not to mess with people like that. He walks into the garage and extends his hand, and in reply, I show him the grease on mine and shrug apologetically.

"You always greet with muck on your hands, boy?" he remarks.

"Not always; you just caught me at a bad time."

Beneath his pierced brows, his eyes are as direct as I expected, not even blinking as much as the average person. But I wasn't scared.

"You sell cars?" he asked.

"No, sir, I just fixed them, and that's it. Why are you looking to buy one?"

"Well, I'm looking for a decent one. I have the cash if you know of any good car dealers nearby?"

"The only one around here is Bob's wheels. I think it's a few miles north from here?"

"Thanks, I will go check that out."

Despite his hard look, he walks out of the garage with no hassle at all. Nonetheless, my life now is different from who I was before. I got my identity changed, a new home, and my own business. Jason really straightened me out and got me back on my feet. The best thing is, I get to keep my first name. Do I regret the past? No. I learn from it, and I feel guilt from it, but I never dwell on it. While I was rummaging through the box of tools my cell phone began to vibrate in my back pocket. That's when I reached for my cell phone and looked at the screen. It was Jason. I haven't heard from him for a few years. I always wondered what happened to him.

"Yeah, what's up big guy?"

"Heard you finally got that Laura girl off your mind?"

"Yeah, moved on, settled down, and completely changed my life man."

He went silent for a moment longer before answering back.

"Listen, Anthony... we need to talk, meet me?"

"Everything all right?"

"I will explain later; I will drop you a message with the location in mind."

He hung up the phone leaving me hanging. I was curious about what he had to tell me.

Nevertheless, I locked up the garage and headed back home to sort out some mess I got myself into, bills were through the roof despite the business bringing in the cash, but it just wasn't paying enough right now. But as I was about to get in my car, I received a text and it read, ***Meet me at Kathy's bar, you know that last place we drank?***

Well, I wasn't going home to clear up my bills, I head right for that bar we last drank. That bar was the place I straightened my head out, so in some strange way, drink solves most problems.

I pulled up outside Kathy's bar, nervous, I didn't know if I was being hooked in for another job or something else, but there is only one way to find out. That's when I switched off the engine to my car and stepped out into the streets of Los Angeles. Everything about this city was beautiful, the buildings, the beach trees, the cars, the women, I mean everything!

Nonetheless, I shut my car door and walk inside Kathy's bar where I stood looking around when I caught sight of Jason waving me over. I walked over and took a seat before him.

"So...what's up man?" I ask.

"Do you want a drink first?"

"I would rather you just come out with it. The suspense is killing me."

He pulls out a light brown envelope and slowly opens it, reaching inside, he slowly pulls out what looked to be a photo of some kid?

"A kid? You brought me all this way for a photo of a kid?"

He placed the photo on the table and gently shoves it towards me and says,

"Not any kid... your kid."

I laughed out loud. I didn't understand what he was saying or what he was trying to do with my head, but he did sort my head out so that's when I realized he isn't the type to take back what he fixed.

I hope not anyway.

"How is this my kid, Jason?"

"I did a little digging with this Laura girl you were madly in love with and found out she has a kid, dates match and the kid looks like you,"

"Yeah, I can see that, but doesn't mean the kid is mine? Why dig up my past?"

"The truth is, I wanted to find out why you were so darn obsessed with her and I saw this kid with her that looks a double of you, I thought you should know, Anthony."

My life went from great and back down to zero. I wasn't sure what I was going to do about this, I froze, speechless to say the least. I guess this just changed the whole gameplay, again.

"What do I do?"

"Well, I do know this, you should make contact with her, the rest is up to you,"

"Maybe I'll have that drink after all,"

"That's my boy!"

I wasn't sure if I was going to contact her, I just sorted my life out and got back on track if not better than ever before. Did I really need to make contact? Would this mess up my new life? This is going to take some thinking, but I do feel my heart is staying away from her, but I could be wrong. I stood up, turned around and walked straight for the door without saying goodbye.

Sitting by the pool on a beach chair with a cold beer looking at my reflection as the water ripples, I couldn't stand the sight of my reflection. I felt I was trapped inside my head deciding on what I should do, but I couldn't make up my mind just yet, I changed myself for the better, although it seemed I was getting feelings back for her again. I was wondering in thoughts, thoughts of contacting her to clear this mystery of a possible child with her. My mood was great before all of this and I was building my life again despite every wrong I did. All this leaves me in a tough position. Do I make contact or just leave it be? It didn't take me - long to snap back to my old ways.

That's when I picked up the cell phone that was beside me on the floor inches away from the beach chair. I had Jason on redial. The phone rang. Jason picked up the phone.

"What's up big bro?" he says.

"Do you have an address?"

"Yeah, and I hope you like flying,"

"What. Why?"

"She is out of the states, bro,"

"Right... now what?"

"Well, now you get on a plane and fly to London."

My heart literally stopped beating for what felt like a minute. I wasn't the type of guy that would be seen on a plain with the amount of news about plane crashes. Everything about planes brought me into a state, and I could feel sick in my stomach just thinking about it.

The thought of heights and going down was not something I liked very much.

"Right... I guess I'm off to London,"

"If you need me, you know where I am. Don't forget about me or I will find you, big bro."

It was clear what I needed to do. That's when I went back inside the house and packed a few belongings.

CHAPTER TWENTY-ONE

The second time stepping into an airport I felt the anxiety was creeping into play like the last time. Knowing I was about to do something I feared the most and that was flying that just made my anxiety worse than usual. While the anxiety was creeping in fast, I began to focus on the number of people that were swarming the airport like a horde of wasps. People could be seen stressing at one another, some were in a panic about missing their flight, and some just lying on the terminal floor that looked as if they had missed their flight. I needed to calm my nerves so I walked towards the airport restaurant before catching my flight to grab a coffee. I was standing in the queue when I saw two cops in front of me looking back at me every few seconds. Right then the only thing I could do was force a smile and a polite nod. That's when they smiled back with the same response, but then one cop could be seen whispering something to his partner that made my anxiety rocket through the roof. I knew that I had to keep my nerves calm before I lost it and give myself away.

I forgot to say that my new name is quite the catch, Anthony West. After the cops were talking amongst each other, that's when they walked away from the queue and walked past me while looking right at me. Sweat began to form and my anxiety was topping over making me feel like I was about to topple over like a tree. Every voice and every motion around me were in slow motion. That's when I passed out causing a scene.

I could feel the water splashing over my face like raindrops and voices calling my name.

"Anthony, can you hear me?"

I could also hear planes flying over and that's when I opened my eyes and panicked.

"I need to catch my flight; I'm going to miss my flight."

I got up from the floor and rushed over to check in for my flight. As I broke into a jog, I looked back to see if the cops were following me, but the cops had gone, and I felt my anxiety beginning to calm. The lady that was behind the desk was about to leave her post and that's when I got desperate.

"I need one ticket to London, please,"

Sir, I am about to go to lunch, but you can wait around for an hour?"

"An hour? Are you joking?"

"I'm sorry, but I really need to go for lunch, sir."

I knew she was determined to pick up her bag and leave for lunch. That's when I needed a story to win her over or I will be waiting a good five hours for the next flight to London.

"My mother is dying."

I squeezed out a few fake tears and broke down right there in front of her hoping she would believe my story. Right then I was thinking about how fucked up my life was. That's what really brought on the tears.

"I...I'm so sorry to hear that. I don't usually do this, but I can see the urgency."

That's when she processed my one-way ticket to London. I was lucky as my plane was seven minutes until it took off, but the lovely lady managed to buy me some time.

"Here you go, sir."

She handed over my ticket and wished me all the best and went for her lunch, and I caught up with my flight just in time. Walking to the terminal I began to calm my nerves despite knowing I was about to board a plane, but in all honesty, I was eager to get on the plane and get this journey over and done with.

It wasn't long before the plane I was on was taking off for London. Sitting close to the window and looking out onto the wing of the plane terrified me, and the man next to me could see that.

"First time flying, right?" the man asks.

"Oh, yeah, first time and the last, obviously when I return it will then be the last." I laugh nervously.

Still looking out the window I began to hear the engines start. I then saw the plane slowly picking up speed along the runway, and that's when the plane took off into the air.

CHAPTER TWENTY-TWO

London international airport was probably the quietest airport I had seen. I wasn't sure what I was going to do on the first night here, although checking into a hotel would be a great start. It was about 8:30 pm walking out of the airport to find a cab, but, luck wasn't on my side as no cabs were around. I found myself waiting around two hours just for a cab. I sat on a bench and began to text Jason to let him know that I had reached London, but... sending failed. My cell phone wasn't set up for international calling or texting. I knew that waiting for a cab could be a while yet so I decided to walk into the city to find somewhere I could stay for at least tonight. I wasn't sure of the prices in London, but I heard there rather expensive.

After knocking on nearly every hotel, B&Bs, and travel lodge, it was clear that there was no place for me to go unless I was willing to sleep in a homeless shelter until morning comes. Facing such a decision, I found myself in a tight situation where I had no choice but to accept the homeless shelter for the night. It's only for one night. As I walked through the door, I felt that my life had been reduced to nothing, only the good side of it all was I had a little cash and that was about it. The sleeping arrangements were not so great. It was just a hall with around a - hundred beds lined up in the centre. It almost looked like something out of a movie where people seek shelter in a pandemic. Nonetheless, there weren't many people here at all, I could easily count eight people including three staff members. Lying on the bed looking up at the ceiling, I began to feel depression creep in because I felt lost, and I missed home.

"You got a light?" a man requested quietly.

"I'm sorry, I packed up smoking years ago," I replied.

The man grunts and rolls over facing away from me. I felt sorry for him even though I didn't know his story.

"You homeless, right?" I ask quietly.

"Yeah, I have been for the last five years. Sleeping rough and hardly any money,"

"Well, where do you get your cash?"

He rolls over facing me and slightly leans forward to me and says,

"I'm not proud of this but I have to steal things to get by and I claim state benefits. It's not much but it gets me by. I need to raise cash so I can get my own place again, I miss those days."

I felt bad for him, and he told me his story until he cried himself to sleep. I couldn't fault him for stealing just so he could survive; because I was in no position to judge anyone. I rolled over facing away as he cries himself to sleep but not without saying,

"Everything we see is temporary, I'm sure things will look up for you one day,"

"I sure hope you are right about that." the man grunts.

"I need to take a walk," I said.

I couldn't sleep with the amount of stuff on my mind. That's why I got up and went straight for the door.

CHAPTER TWENTY-THREE

As the day turns to night, Laura was cooking dinner for her four-year-old son, Kyle. It was 9:00 pm at night she stood there cooking a little later than usual because they had been travelling across London on an adventure that Kyle was so excited to do. Laura seemed in a little state of panic because she was due to go to work in a few hours, but she had so much to do before she could leave. Her babysitter was giving her the run around saying she couldn't make it and then saying she could. That left Laura in an awkward position where she debated whether to phone into work to say she wasn't coming in. That's when the doorbell rang just as she was dishing up dinner.

"Great, now she decides to turn up."

Laura placed the food on the table and went straight to the front door. She opens the door and her babysitter Lisa stood before her and says,

"You have no idea what it's like for a woman in a pub on their own," Lisa explained.

Laura laughs but really thinks about how much of a mess around she really is.

"Sorry to hear that. Are you staying to take care of Kyle while I head to work in a few hours?"

"Yeah, that's why I'm here, silly."

Lisa is twenty-five years old claiming benefits and working for Laura for a little pin money just so she could get by. Lisa was always involved with men that just about gave her a bad name. Some guys call her outdated meat, also known as, Sket. Lisa was still standing there looking rather paranoid when Laura says,

"Are you OK?"

"Yeah… I think so?"

"Come inside," Laura says,

Lisa walks inside and Laura began to slowly shut the door when she saw a man walking past her gate with his hood up. The man stopped; looking back at Laura every few seconds, but she could not work out the face. As Laura shut the door, Lisa noticed a look on Laura's face.

"You OK, Laura?"

"I think so?"

She paused for a moment and said,

"It's nothing."

Laura walked back into the kitchen while Lisa walked into the living room where Kyle could be seen sitting on the sofa playing on his portable computer. For a four-year-old, he played it well despite his young age. Lisa takes a seat next to Kyle and says,

"Hey, Kyle," she says in a soft tone.

He slightly turns his head and lost concentration playing his game but smiled and just started his game again.

"Lisa, could you come and help me in here please, I seem to mess things up."

Lisa stood from sitting and walks into the kitchen to lend a hand.

"Are you sure you're OK, Laura?"

"Yeah, I just have an hour until work and some guy outside stared back at me a few times,"

"It's probably nothing to worry about, Laura,"

"Probably. You are right I may be overreacting."

Laura grabbed her keys, bag, and coat and rushed into the living room to give Kyle a kiss before she left for work.

"You be a good boy, Kyle,"

"He will be a gem, Laura, don't worry,"

"You are so right, but please lock the door and don't answer it."

"I won't. Anyway, get going before you are late, Laura."

Laura heads for the door, but before she went on her way she looks back and listens to Kyle giggling away. That to her was the comfort she needed to hear, that Kyle was in fact in safe hands.

The streets were blackened by the night despite the streetlamps giving a little light. Laura had been walking to work because she didn't like the bus ride at this time of night. London night buses were rowdy and the last time she went on the bus to work she had been sandwiched by two drunk men that were making her life uneasy. While she had been walking to work, Laura had taken the back streets because she felt safe that way. But something didn't feel right to her. Laura had taken a wrong turn into a dark alleyway when she saw a woman in distress shouting. Four men in hoodies were beating a young girl that looked to be in her twenties, but as Laura took one step back away from the men; she had been spotted. That's when she turns around to leave but suddenly two other men jump in front of her and began walking slowly towards her. Laura was in deep trouble, and yet, she had no way out of that sticky situation.

CHAPTER TWENTY-FOUR

If it wasn't for Laura's babysitter shouting her mouth off in a bar, I wouldn't be here now to save her from a beating or worse. I could clearly see she was in distress when I guy in a hoodie grabbed her from behind and the other two walked slowly towards her brandishing a knife. I kept watching behind a bin waiting for that moment. While I was waiting, I could see the fourth man slowly slicing through the woman's neck and forcing Laura to watch as he did it. They all laugh as the woman was choking on her own blood. It didn't phase me because I have done much worse things to people. After watching, I could see the fourth man stand from kneeling on the floor, brushing the dirt from his knees, and then wiping the knife across his right knee.

"Your turn, sweetheart."

He slowly walks towards her but takes his time. I knew what he was doing, he wanted to seriously give her the fright of her life before he ends her. That's when I needed to act, that is very soon. The three men threw Laura to the ground and started spitting at her as she buried her head in the ground to protect her face. That's when I made my move. I didn't make a sound as I moved swiftly towards one guy, snapping his neck from behind, and swiftly moving toward the next guy, but he managed to tackle me to the ground.

That's when I could see the other two kicking Laura, repeatedly in the stomach. While I was wrestling with this guy that was on top of me, choking the hell out of me, I heard a gunshot cut through the alleyway. The guy that was on top of me; fell off me, and all I could see was Laura holding the gun, but she looked right at me and pulled the trigger.

BANG, BANG, BANG.

All I heard was the last shell dropping to the floor, that's when my vision blurred and all I could see was Laura running away, but I had to do something to stop her, that may be my last chance to put things right.

"LAURA, PLEASE, WAIT!" I shout.

She stopped. It had taken her a few minutes before she turns around to face what she had done to me.

"Anthony, no, it can't be?"

She slowly turns around but paused momentarily before running over to me. She runs back over to me seeing me laying in my own blood. She was in shock, scared of the outcome of what might be. I could see it on her face. I wasn't scared of dying, I was more scared of leaving her behind, and my time left with her being so short.

"Why are you here?" she asked.

She leans down and that made it clear for me to see the tears run down her left cheek and hit the ground. The pain in her eyes was nothing that I saw before that night she was at the motel. This pain she was feeling was far more intense.

"I heard you had a son and I thought they would be a chance that he would be mine. That's why I'm here. I followed you."

I was coughing up blood and really feeling like I was about to fall asleep right there in front of her. But as I was lying here looking deep into her eyes, I felt I needed to tell her the truth. I felt I needed to explain everything to her. I couldn't die leaving her without the truth about her best friend, Kate or the fact that I had killed everyone that got close to her, but for now, I wanted answers before I leave this world.

"I guess I really thought I could maybe get another shot with you, I guess I blew that one." I laughed.

That's when Laura could be seen punching in the numbers for the emergency services.

Laura had cradled Anthony in her arms while waiting for the emergency services to pick up the phone, but Anthony knew he couldn't go on like this. He reached for her phone and took it away from her hands and hung up.

"Anthony, no, what are you doing?"

That's when she began kissing his forehead, begging him to allow her to help him. He didn't want help. He wanted to help her with answers.

"Look, Laura, see, I have something to tell you and after I tell you, I believe you would regret calling for help."

Her eyes filled up. She was ready to burst into tears again, and she did.

"Tell me what?" a soft tone in her voice.

"Kate, your friend, right? Well, I was the one that killed her and the others too."

Laura looks deep into his eyes, but too slowly to be normal. When she speaks her voice trails slowly like her words are unwilling to take flight. There is sadness in her eyes.

"W-what!"

Her brain had shut down. She was clammy and there was the glisten of a cold sweat. Her eyes were as wide as if someone was coming to deliver a bullet. Yet, what she saw, no one else could see. Trapped in her own psychosis, a living nightmare for one, tailor-made by Anthony. She was confused and scared, but unable to move. She wanted more answers.

"Go on." she insisted.

"I told you I love you and that makes me unlovable. I said that I care and that makes me the target of your hatred. I brought you gifts and poured affection into your life and you attacked me over and over. You left me with a heart that explodes in my chest. I would still be your friend if you would accept what I did, but I know that you won't."

The sirens wailed like a baby in distress, the kind of noise that makes you sick.

Laura looks at Anthony and gave him a soft and gentle kiss on his lips and says,

"Kyle is your son, Anthony."

"I love you, Laura,"

"I loved you."

Anthony felt at ease and smiled.

"You should go because the police will be here any minute now."

Laura made a snap decision and left in a hurry, but she looked back only once and she was gone, out of sight.

A few minutes passed and someone could be seen lurking around the dark alleyway where Anthony was dying. Anthony couldn't work out the face but only the body shape of a mysterious woman.

"Who are you, show yourself," he remarks.

The echo of footsteps could be heard getting closer towards Anthony. The sound of the footsteps could only be female.

She gets even closer now, inches away from where Anthony could be seen lying in a pool of his blood. She stands over him slowly removing her hood that was hiding her face, then says,

"You know we could have been so fitting together, Anthony. You taught me how to be a woman and a killer. I think killing my landlord woke me up, I feel alive again,"

"Laura, you were dead?" he replies.

"You assume too much, the truth is, I was following you all along because I love you."

"Well, I'm dying now so your luck has gone,"

"Maybe."

Laura kneels to Anthony kissing him softly on his lips and whispers.

"She will pay for this."

She picks up the gun that was inches away from him and places it in his hands and says,

"Go out with a bang."

Laura stands back up and slowly walks away with a wicked laugh but Anthony pulls the trigger on her, bringing her to her knees.

He knows he has done wrong and the only way he could make it right was to eliminate everything he had created, leaving Laura Edwards to be free once more.

DELUSION THE LOVE OF MY LIFE

Thank you for reading Delusion the love of my life. Please don't forget to leave this book a review as this helps others decide if this book is right for them. Thank you, again.